TOCABAGA 3

WARM BLOOD – COLD STEEL

THOMAS H. WARD

TOCABAGA 3:

Warm Blood – Cold Steel

THE TOCABAGA CHRONICLES

by

THOMAS H. WARD

ISBN-13: 978-0615939339

ISBN-10: 0615939333

Transcendent Publishing
121 104th Ave. Treasure Island, FL 33706
www.transcendentpublishing.com

I am the oldest of three Brothers. We grew up fighting bullies and gang members in a tough neighborhood in south Chicago. My Dad, one of the most honest men I have known, stressed to me to always tell the truth and help each other. Never ever be a bully, never steal, and try to protect those who cannot protect themselves. I have always stood up for the people who could not defend themselves. I hate liars and bullies.

Standing 6 feet tall at 180 pounds, I am in great shape for my age and my body is honed by years of physical training. I keep in shape by lifting weights almost every day and running three miles four times a week. I shave my head two times a week as it is cooler with no hair in the hot south and wear a ball hat to keep the sun off my head. I sport a gray mustache and goatee that I keep well trimmed and short.

There is a 2 inch scar on my forehead from a

knife fight years ago. I spent four years in the Army as a Military Policeman, and became an expert in the use of handguns, rifles, shotguns, and hand-to-hand combat. My legs have skin grafts from burns due to an explosion when I worked for the DOD (Department of Defense) doing security work for seven years. I always carry my Glock 17 side arm and Black Bear Cold Steel fighting knife no matter where I go.

I love our country, freedom, my family, and friends. If anyone messes with my family, or my friends justice will be swift and painful. I have no use for anyone who breaks the law, cheats or steals. For the most part I follow the Ten Commandments, but also believe in The Code of Hammurabi which is an eye for an eye. I fight to keep our Bill of Rights under the United States Constitution. That is me, Jack Gunn, a.k.a. Tocabaga Jack and these are my chronicles.

I am Director of Security for Tocabaga Island. I live here along with 556 other Patriots, we are fighting to keep our freedom, keep our homes, and keep our families safe from the evil forces gone wild. Tocabaga is a sanctuary or safe haven, if you believe in the Constitution, the Bill of Rights, and are of good moral character you are welcome here.

We are waiting for you to contact us by email to find out where Tocabaga is located. Sending us an email is your first step to Freedom. There is an email address hidden in these chronicles. Tocabaga is a real location. I will reply.

Jack Gunn

MAY 15, 2025

I received a phone call from Colonel Turner the Army Ranger Commanding Officer, "Jack just to let you know what is going on. We still have not located Captain Sessions. It's strange because we have three methods to locate someone. One is by the cell phone location, another by the electronic dog tags and all officers have a body implant which gives off a signal good for 5 miles.

"Now here is the strange part, his phone and dog tags were found miles away from the church where he went missing, but the implant signal is coming from inside the church. Twenty men searched every inch of that church and found nothing. Jack, do you have any ideas and do you know anything about that area? We are stumped."

I glanced at my watch, it was 7 am. Because of the rain yesterday it is humid and hot today. Yesterday May 14th Captain Sessions went MIA or missing in action while fighting al-Qaida about three miles from here at an old church. It is believed that church was the al-Qaida headquarters.

"Colonel, that is very weird. If he was captured they may have cut out his implant. How big is this thing?"

"It is about the size of a pin head so it would be hard to find if someone cut it out of his body and threw it somewhere. The implants are supposed to be top secret. I hope al-Qaida doesn't know about them."

"Can they be detected with a metal detector and where are they located on the body?"

"They are injected into the right side of your abdominal area. They can be detected by a metal scanner."

"Colonel, is the church still a hot area?"

"Yes it is, as soon as you come off of Tocabaga the whole area is hot as al-Qaida snipers are all over the place. I think it is going to take another three days to get this area under full control. If I had to guess I would say there were about 2,000 al-Qaida fighters located here, we under estimated them. I don't know how many we have killed."

"Wow 2,000 is incredible! Colonel if you agree I would like to help search for Captain Sessions today. I know that area and I attended that church once. I would like to bring eight men and Rahim with me."

"Rahim, why do you want to bring him? He isn't a shooter."

"Right he isn't a shooter but he is a Muslim and he knows more than we do about how these guys think. Rahim was good friends with Aamir."

"Ok Jack, you have my permission when you get ready to leave give me a call. After you call me I will notify the check points you are coming. What color trucks are you driving."

"We will have two trucks, one blue Ford and one black Ford F250. We'll be there by 0930 hours."

"Roger that Jack, see you then. I'll be here until we find Sessions. No one gets left behind. We will not rest until we find Captain Sessions, one way or another."

"Bye Colonel."

My wife asked, "What is going on?"

"We need to go search for Captain Sessions, he is missing in action or MIA."

3

"So you are going to be the searchers."

"Yup, we are The Searchers."

The searchers, it reminded me of the movie "The Searchers" starring John Wayne. The Indians kidnapped a little girl and Wayne spent five years looking for her. He would never give up until he found her. It was one of my favorite movies.

I told her the whole story of how Sessions was in a gun battle and four of his men were killed; and he just disappeared. Then I got on the radio to everyone who was on the search team advising them to meet at the bridge at 0900 hours wearing full body armor. Our ammo and gear were already loaded from yesterday and we were ready to go.

As Tommy, Ron, Jim Bo, and I left the house our wives gave us a kiss and wished us good luck. I could tell they were worried and not happy we were going into harms' way to help find Captain Sessions. Finding Captain Sessions was the primary objective but finding the al-Qaida money that maybe hidden at the church was our second goal.

Our search team was made up of the best shooters. We have Tommy, Eddy, Rick, Chris, Tony, Ron, Jim Bo and me. Rahim would be along for translations and since he was close friends with Aamir maybe he can provide some insight to our search.

We stopped to talk to Rahim. I had not asked him to go with us yet. I didn't know if he would come along or not, but thought he would like to help out to show his appreciation for saving his family.

Knocking on his door he answered, "Hello guys, how can I help you?"

I replied, "Rahim we need your help. Captain Sessions was at the church on 54th Ave and went missing yesterday. Do you know the church called the United Church of Christ?"

"Yes I do, one time I went with my wife to service there. It is a nice church or use to be. So what do you want me to do?"

"Captain Sessions believed that was the headquarters for al-Qaida and he went to check it out. There was a big gun battle, four Ranges were killed, and he went missing. The Colonel tracked him and believes he is in the church area but no one can find him."

"That's not good; if al-Qaida has him then it is really bad."

"Right, so we need you to help us search. We are also looking for any funds that al-Qaida may have hidden there. Since you knew Aamir better than anyone else maybe, just maybe, you would have a better idea where he would hide any funds."

"Funds, you mean money?"

"Yes money, gold or whatever."

"Ok when do we go?"

"We'll leave in one hour. Tommy will get you a bullet proof vest to wear. Be at the bridge in one hour by 9 am."

"Ok Jack it is my pleasure to help you in any way possible."

It was 8:45 am and kick off time was 9:00 am. Everyone was there waiting for Rahim. He came trotting down the road and Tommy handed him the largest bullet proof vest we had, it barely fit his 6' 4" frame.

As we were standing there I told everyone, "This is a dangerous mission. First and foremost we need to find Captain Sessions. The second objective is to find any al-Qaida cache. If we are lucky maybe we find both at the same time. Let's say a prayer before we leave."

We stood in a circle holding hands and I prayed, "God please give us the strength, courage, and guidance to find our brother Captain Sessions. Please watch over us and protect us from evil, Amen."

Everyone, even Rahim said, "Amen."

We had on full body armor and each man carried 300 rounds of ammo. The four people who were assigned security while we are at the church were Tony, Tommy, Chris, and Rick. Two of them would carry SAWS and extra ammo would be in our trucks. The other two had M 4 carbines with scopes.

Ron, Jim Bo, Eddy, and I would do the actual searching along with Rahim. Jim Bo and Eddy carried the metal detectors and all of us carried M 4 carbines. In addition everyone carried a hand gun of some type. My side arm of choice is a Glock 17 which is a 9 mm and it has a 17 round magazine. I never go anywhere without my 8 inch double edge Black Bear Cold Steel Bowie knife strapped to my tactical vest.

I shouted out, "Let's go."

I was driving my old 1997 Ford Expedition with a 5.4 liter motor. I love this truck as it has 2 wheel drive, all wheel drive, 4 wheel high, and 4 wheel low. I think 1997 was the only year they made that drive system. It takes a licking and keeps on ticking. The other truck was a 2008 4x4 Ford F 250 pickup, turbo diesel with big tires. It was jacked up about 6 inches for added ground clearance.

Riding in my truck was Ron, Tommy, Rahim, Jim Bo, and I was driving. In the other truck Tony was driving, along with Chris, Eddy, and Rick. Each truck had one SAW light machine gun. As we left Camp Tocabaga the guards at the bridge wished us good luck. None of us said a word.

I phoned Colonel Turner, "We are on the way, and we just left Tocabaga."

"Ok Jack the church area is under control, so proceed."

"Roger that Colonel."

As we approached the first check point located at the first main intersection we were amazed at the destruction, every building was in shambles, some completely destroyed, and others had big ass holes blown in them. The once expensive buildings were piles of smoking rubble. The Abrams tank destroyed everything. I was surprised we didn't see any dead al-Qaida fighters.

We stopped at the check point where eight Rangers were standing next to a Humvee short for HMMWV (High Mobility Multipurpose Wheeled Vehicle) with a 50 caliber machine gun mounted on the roof. Sergeant Smith approached our trucks and asked me, "Are you guys crazy coming here?"

I said, "Yes we are, crazy in love with you Army guys. I hope we can find Captain Sessions."

"We hope you can as well. There are three more check points down the road; one at the bridge, one at the toll booth, and one at the intersection of 34th Street and 54th Avenue. Once you leave here keep up your speed to around 60 mph so snipers will have a hard time shooting your trucks. Don't stop at any point too long or they can get a bead on you."

"Sergeant Smith did you guys kill anyone? Where are all the bodies?"

"We killed hundreds of them and we all ready

dumped the bodies. Others are buried in the rubble."

"Ok, thanks Sergeant."

The Rangers half raised their hands as if giving a wave as we pulled away making a right turn on Bayway Drive. I punched the accelerator to the floor to get up to 65 mph. The Bayway is also the same as 54th Ave when you come to 34th street. It is a four lane divided road all the way to the church.

I asked Tommy, "What did Smith mean we dumped the bodies?"

"I don't have any idea ... it just means they got rid of them somehow and I don't care how."

"I agree who gives a shit. Maybe they fed them to the sharks like we do."

"Yep we are sure getting a lot of sharks around here because we feed them all the time."

Everyone in the truck was laughing when all of a sudden we heard a loud BANG, it sounded like a rock hitting the truck but it was a bullet hitting the side of the truck and every one ducked down. We didn't see where it came from and I was just happy it didn't hit a tire. Getting a flat tire in a sniper zone could get one of us killed. I floored it after I heard the bang, speeding up to

85 mph, trying to get away from the sniper fire.

I yelled, "Is everyone ok? Where the hell did that bullet hit us?"

Jim Bo answered, "I think the right rear fender. We're all ok."

Approaching the second check point the Rangers just waved us pass. We didn't slow down much and zoomed thru raising our hands to say thank you.

I looked in my mirror and Tony was about 20 car lengths behind us. That was good because if he was too close it would make an easier target to hit. In a minute we'll be going past the college, speeding by it we heard gun fire and could see Army Rangers all over the place along with the Abrams Tank the Iron Maiden.

Eddy was on the radio and said, "Jack they are shooting at us. We've been hit several times but nothing serious."

Tommy replied back, "Of course they are shooting at us you fool. Just keep your head down. Do you have on your Depends?"

The other day Eddy shit his pants when an al-Qaida fighter almost killed him so we told him to wear

Depends. It seemed funny at the time.

To shoot a pickup truck going 60 mph is not easy to do. You have to be a good shooter and be at the correct distance. Lucky for us al-Qaida snipers were not good shooters. We zoomed ahead to the final check point at 34th street. The Rangers flagged us down, and I stomped on the brakes coming to a tire screeching stop.

One Ranger, Sergeant Jones came up to my truck and advised, "Colonel Turner is expecting you guy's. Do you know where to go?"

"Yes, we do Sergeant Jones."

"Ok Jack it's just down the road here about half a mile on the left side. Be careful because after this point it is no man's land."

"Right, thanks."

Taking off I spun the tires burning some rubber. Pulling up to the church we saw about fifty Rangers in different positions around the area. Parked in the church yard was the Bradley fighting vehicle Gun Smoke. Seeing Gun Smoke there made me feel a little more secure.

Colonel Turner came up as we got out of the trucks and commented, "I see you made it here in one piece. Did you take any sniper hits?"

"Yes we took one round in the fender and the other truck maybe two rounds." We walked around each truck checking out the damage. They were just bullet holes that went thru the side of truck causing no serious damage.

Turner said, "Come on inside the church and take a look."

The church is an "L" shaped building, single story with cathedral ceilings about 20 feet high. It is an old building built around 1970. The grounds around it are open except for a few trees and over grown bushes making the area look like a jungle.

No one lived in the homes around this area. People had long ago moved away for safety reasons when the gangs made it too dangerous. I assumed most moved to the Green Zone downtown were the police would protect them and they could obtain food. When you move to the Green Zone you become a slave of the state and must follow ever order they give you.

The inside of the church is open with bare walls and a tile floor. It had about eight offices or rooms that were empty now. Just looking at the rooms there are not many places to hide anything. We went to the chapel room and the pews were still there but a big cross was on the floor broken into pieces; a picture of Jesus was torn up lying there in a crumbled heap.

I told Jim Bo and Eddy who carried the metal detectors, "Start doing a sweep of every inch of the floors and when the floors are done do the walls."

"Ok Jack but it will take about 3 or 4 hours to do that," replied Eddy.

"I don't care if it takes a month; we are looking for a tiny pin head size piece of metal or anything not normal. The rest of us will visually scan the floors and also check the walls for anything unusual. Look for anything that maybe different in appearance."

After about two hours Jim Bo yelled out, "I think this is blood on the floor. It's hard to tell because the tiles are dark gray."

We all converged on the spot. I was shining a bright light on it and it sure looked like a dried blood spot. It was about three feet in diameter, I touched it with my index finger, and it was slightly tacky meaning it wasn't fresh blood.

I told Jim Bo, "Scan this area good and don't

miss an inch."

As Jim Bo was scanning the detector gave off a very slight beep. We all stopped and pulled out flash lights shining them at a three foot area.

Colonel Turner said, "Look, here's a small crack!"

There was a very small crack in the tile grout. A crack that the pin head size implant could fit into. Ron ran out to get a hammer and chisel from the truck. Coming back he began to hammer the tile breaking it up in small pieces around the grout line. We were all standing there shining our lights and Ron picked up something showing it to Colonel Turner and asked, "Is this it?"

We all huddled around trying to get a view and Turner looking at it said, "Yes that's it."

Eddy said, "Dam that thing is small. How does it work?"

Turner advised, "I don't know how it works exactly but it gives off some kind of signal which can be detected by our drones."

I replied, "This means Sessions isn't here and the funds aren't here either."

I asked Rahim, "What do you think?"

Rahim said, "This is not a place that Aamir would use to hide any person or funds in my opinion."

"Then what kind of place do you think Aamir would use?"

"Thinking back, Aamir hated Catholics but liked their churches. He liked the Catholic Church down the road because it has an excellent building design. One time we went there together just to look around. It is the Blessed Trinity Church about a mile from here. I suggest we search there."

Turner commented, "My Rangers have not cleared that area yet. If we go there it will be dangerous."

We all looked at each other waiting for someone to speak so I jumped in, "Look we searched every inch of this church and know that Captain Sessions is not here. I suggest we go to the Blessed Trinity now there's no time to waste. I've been to that church a few times with my brother and his wife. It is a big church with a lot of rooms and it has a house next to it for the Priests and another building for storage."

Turner replied, "Ok I agree, my men will go in

first with Gun Smoke and clear the church buildings. I will leave eight men here for a check point leaving us forty men for the operation."

I looked at my watch it was almost 2 pm we needed to get going.

Colonel Turner gathered everyone and assigned his men into four teams, one for breaching each building, all to be breached at the same time, and one team for security watch along with Gun Smoke. Our team "The Searchers" would be the last ones to enter any building.

Turner advised us, "Jack wait here until I radio you to come to the church. This area seems to be safe for now. It may take us an hour or so to clear the buildings. So stay here and be on your toes."

"Ok Colonel we'll wait for your call."

The Rangers mounted up and sped down the road at what seemed like full speed. They wanted to move in fast and hard, taking any al-Qaida there by surprise.

They left and all was very still, no noise just the wind blowing. I posted my men to watch for any movement and stay alert. The eight Rangers were standing on the main road next to their Humvee with a 50 caliber mounted machine gun, ready to stop any car coming down the road. There was no traffic on the road so if you saw a car or truck most likely it was not a friend.

I was sitting in my truck with Tommy and Ron. We had the doors open and windows down because it was hot as usual. We were parked on the side street next to the church near some bushes. I was eating an orange and as I looked up there was a face in the bushes about hundred feet away. I looked closer at the face threw my rifle scope.

It was a little kid looking at us. I wondered what the hell is a kid is doing here. He just stared at us not making a move. Putting down my M 4, I waved at him to come over. He started to come out from behind the bushes. I watched him slowly approach, making sure he did not have any weapons or bombs.

I said, "Guys we got company a little kid is coming over to us."

Tommy looked up, racked a round into his M 4, and replied, "A little kid, what the hell is he doing here?"

The little boy was about 10 years old. He looked skinny, he was dirty, his shirt was dirty, and his jeans had holes in the knees. He had light brown hair and was a good looking kid. I sat there watching this little boy walking up to us in this dangerous area.

I pulled my Glock out and put it on my seat just in case. Tommy and Ron jumped out of the truck, watching the whole area for anyone else that might pop up.

Walking slowly up to me, stopping about ten feet away, the little kid said in a whisper, "Hey Mister, are you with the Army?"

"Hi little man, yes we are with the Army. Are you by yourself?"

"No I have a little brother, we live over there." He pointed to a house about 200 feet away.

I got out of the truck and he backed away from me, keeping his distance, showing he was scared of us. I reached in the truck grabbed an orange and tossed it to him which he caught showing good reflexes.

"Thanks Mister, can I have one for my brother?"

I tossed him another one and asked him, "What

19

can we do for you?"

"We have an Army guy hidden at my house and he needs help. Come on I'll show you."

Tommy said, "Dad this could be a trap."

I asked the kid, "What's your name?"

"Johnny Evans and my brother is Jimmy Evans."

"Where are your Dad and Mom?"

"The bad guys with towels over their heads killed my Mom and Dad. They came into our house and my Dad told us to hide. My brother and I have a special hiding place, no one knows where it is, my Dad made it."

"Sorry about your Mom and Dad Johnny.

"What is the Army man's name?"

"I think its Captain something. That's what he told me."

"Tommy and Ron get everyone; we're going to his house. Captain Sessions has to be there.

"Ok Johnny, take us to your house."

We followed little Johnny as he weaved around the bushes sneaking along stealth like. He did not follow the road or walk out in the open. This little kid knew what he was doing. As we approached the house Johnny opened a side window and crawled in. Tommy and I followed and the others stayed outside.

Winding room to room in the house we came to a closet in the hall and Johnny opened the door. Tommy and I had our guns at the ready not knowing what to expect. With the door open we saw clothes hanging there, it was a small closet, and no one could fit in there. Then Johnny pushed the clothes aside showing a bare wall, he reached down and picked up part of the floor, it was a trap door.

Johnny said, "Go look he is down there with my brother."

I pulled out my flash light and my Glock 17 just in case and jumped down into the hole it was only a four foot drop. A strong odor came from the room it smelled like urine, crap, and blood. I kneeled down shining my light into the dark and saw a little kid holding a candle to provide some light in this concrete lined little room. I guessed the room size was 10 x 10 feet in size.

I told the kid, "Jimmy don't be afraid your brother Johnny is here with us. We're with the Army.

We're the good guys."

Huddled in the corner holding his candle he answered, "I am glad you are good guys."

Shinning my light around I saw him lying there, it was Captain Sessions, bloody but alive, and Sessions mumbled, "What the hell took you guys so long."

"Captain, are you able to move?"

"I can crawl but can't walk. I took a round in the leg and I think it's broke along with my collar bone. They beat me up pretty good but I could be dead."

"Come on Captain let's get out of here. Tommy come down here and help me carry Sessions out."

We dragged him out and pulled out little Jimmy who was about seven years old. He looked just like his brother.

I got on the horn to Colonel Turner, "We located Captain Sessions he is alive but wounded and will need a chopper and medical help."

"Holy crap Jack! Where did you find him?"

"He was in a house directly behind the church. A little kid named Johnny saved his life."

"We already checked that house and all the others around that area. Tell Sessions the chopper is on the way. I will be there shortly."

"Roger that Colonel."

Out in the light Captain Sessions looked pretty bad, but lucky for him the leg wound was not bleeding, it looked like the bullet went in broke the bone and came back out. His face and head were badly bruised and he had two black eyes.

We had Sessions on a homemade stretcher, a blanket. Everyone there came over to shake his hand. I gave him some water and Johnny peeled him an orange with an old rusty pocket knife. I looked at Johnny and thought what a good kid. He took care of Sessions and his brother. He was a Hero in my mind.

I asked Johnny, "How did you find Captain Sessions?"

"We saw the bad guys all leave the church so I sneaked inside looking for some food and found him tied up on the floor. I cut the ropes with my knife and he was free. The Captain cut something out of his side with my knife and then I helped him to my house to hide. We all hid in the room when the bad guys came back looking for him."

"Well Johnny you are a hero. Let me see your

knife. I see it's a little rusty. I want you to have my pocket knife. This is a very important knife it belonged to one of my best friends who was also killed by bad guys."

As I handed him Marks fishing knife he replied, "Gee Mister thanks a lot, it's a great looking knife."

"Be careful it's very sharp."

"Yes Sir, I'll be careful."

Little Jimmy watching asked, "Can I have a knife?" Johnny handed him his old rusty knife and Jimmy was happy as a pig in the mud.

I told them, "My name is Jack Gunn."

They replied, "Yes Sir, Mr. Gunn."

I thought what well manner kids they are, their parents would be proud of them. We have to get these kids out of here, out of danger and take them to Tocabaga. I like these boys and want to adopt them into my family since they have no one else to help them. I have to take them back to Tocabaga now.

Colonel Turner came down the road in his Humvee and stopped next to Sessions. He shook his hand and whispered something in his ear. Just then we heard the Black Hawk UH 60 coming in to land in the street. With the blades still spinning the Rangers loaded Captain Sessions on board and it took off toward SOCOM HQ located in Tampa, where Sessions could obtain proper medical help.

We obtained our major objective which was to find Captain Sessions. I looked at my watch it was 5 pm and in a few hours it would be dark. That's no time to be out here. We would have to come back tomorrow to search the other church. I wanted to get these kids out of danger.

I commented, "Colonel Turner this is Johnny Evans and his brother Jimmy. They saved Captain Sessions."

Turner shook hands with both boys and said, "On behalf of the United States Army Rangers thank you for your service to your country boys. You did a brave deed. Where are your parents?"

Johnny answered, "They were both killed by the bad guys."

"Oh I'm sorry Johnny. You are safe with us and I am sure Mr. Gunn will take good care of you."

Looking at me Johnny said, "Mr. Gunn can we come with you when you leave?"

"Johnny how would you and your brother like to come live with me on Tocabaga Island. It is safe there and we have a lot of food."

"You mean stay with you."

"Yes with me and my family."

"Yes Sir, that sounds great."

Turner advised, "We have cleared the church buildings but I think it is too late for you to do any searching for al-Qaida funds. Jack I have to give you a lot of credit for finding Captain Sessions. We owe you and your men a lot. You have our upmost respect."

"Colonel you owe us nothing, we all owe Johnny and little Jimmy a lot for saving Captain Sessions. If you agree we are heading back to Tocabaga with the kids and we'll come back to search the church tomorrow."

"Jack, I agree we will post men at the church tonight so tomorrow you can go there knowing it's safe. Give me a call when you are leaving Camp Tocabaga."

"Thank you Colonel."

We made it back to Tocabaga with no problems. I introduced the boys to their new family. Hemmi, my wife, was very happy to have little boys around. It made me feel really good that we saved two little kids from the jaws of death. I need to do more searching; I need to save more kids from a terrible life.

Shanda and Kendra were happy to have new play mates and showed the boys around the house.

Johnny and Jimmy ate more food than two grown men could. They loved the baked fish, fruit, and rice. It seems they like their bedroom and new home. I would see that Johnny and Jimmy got a medal for saving Captain Sessions.

It was late so Hemmi and I took the kids to their bedroom where they took a shower and washed up. We tucked them into bed. Johnny held his new knife tight in his hand as he fell asleep.

I decided I would go back to their house and see what I could find to bring them, like toys or pictures of their parents. I also wondered what happened to their parent's bodies so we would look for them.

Later that night I got a phone call from Captain Sessions advising he would be out of action for only a few months according to the Doctor. Maybe someday he will tell us the story of what happen to him.

Tomorrow we will go back to the church and search for the al-Qaida cache.

MAY 16, 2025

As stated in my earlier chronicles, the United States is in a state of chaos, and extreme turmoil. We came to this because of an overzealous President and a Congress that sat by and did nothing to protect our rights.

The President put into effect Presidential Executive Order 13603 which to everyone's surprise declares that all property belongs to the Federal government, your house, money, guns, and even your kids. They can tell you where to live and where to work.

Years before things were not making much sense especially when the government took control of the news media. It became state owned so the only news we received was what the Federal government wanted us to see.

Back in 2013 the NSA started to tap our phones, reading our emails, reading our snail mail, reading our face book page. We were all being watched, we were all suspected of doing something wrong, we were all having our Bill of Rights violated in the name of government security, and no one did anything about it.

Benjamin Franklin once said, "He who sacrifices freedom for security deserves neither."

Thank God the US Military believes Executive Order 13603 violates the US Constitution. The Army Rangers are fighting with us to gain control back from the Federal Police, al-Qaida, and numerous gangs. We will win this fight, we will never surrender, and we will persevere.

I woke up early as usual it was 5 a.m. and made a cup of coffee then went out for a smoke. I need a smoke to wake up with a cup of strong coffee. It seems to be a habit I can't break. I don't smoke around the kids. I get my cigarettes from the Rangers who seem to have an endless supply.

Looking at my phone I had an email message sent to tocabaga.jack@gmail.com from Colonel Turner it read, "Call me when you are ready to leave."

I went to check on the boys in their bedroom. They were sleeping sound as a rock. I noticed that Johnny still had Marks' knife in his hand. This maybe the first time in months they had good food and a good nights' sleep without worry. Johnny had to have a lot of stress on him watching over Sessions and his little brother. Taking care of them, getting them water, and food to eat. I thought this kid is special.

Looking at Johnny and Jimmy I didn't want to go searching for anything. I wanted to stay here and spend some time with them. I felt that was important to do since this was their new home. Maybe we can play baseball when I return.

Hemmi woke up and I made her a cup of coffee like I always do and I asked her, "Please pay special attention to the boys since this is their new home."

Hemmi said, "Don't worry Jack I know how to take care of kids better than you. They will feel right at home."

"I know Honey you're the best."

I went to take a shower while she cooked breakfast. It was the usual fried fish and oranges. Tommy, Ron, and Jim Bo woke up and joined me for breakfast.

Tonya, my son's wife asked, "Are you going back to the church today?"

Tommy replied, "Yes we're going to search for the funds."

My brother's wife Joan said, "What for, it is not worth risking your lives."

I commented, "Well we also need to go back to the house Johnny lived in and bury his Mom and Dad. I want to bring back any items such as toys, and pictures. These kids saved Captain Sessions and we owe them a lot."

Joan answered back, "I guess you are right."

"Johnny took care of Sessions and his little brother; he is a hero in my eyes. He is a smart little kid and very well mannered. So please, all of you take special care of them and show them around Tocabaga. They are part of our family now. We are all they have."

"Don't worry Jack we know how to take care of kids," replied Joan.

It seemed I just heard that statement. No one else said a word. All the men got up and left to go outside. I got on the radio to the others advising to meet at 9 am at the bridge.

The same team showed up at the bridge and we all shook hands. We were proud about finding Captain

Sessions. I felt we could accomplish any mission no matter what it was. I told everyone we were going to the kids' house to find their dead parents and bury them. I also advised them I want to bring back any toys and pictures so we need to search the house. After that we'll go to the church to look for the loot.

As we were talking Amy, Johnny, and Jimmy came running up to us and Amy said, "Johnny wants to ask you something."

Johnny said, "Sir if you go to my house will you bring us our baseball gloves, baseball, and bat. They are in our bedroom."

I said, "Yes Johnny is there anything else you want?"

"We got a toy box could you please bring that too?"

"Ok Johnny we will bring everything. Are there any other kids living near your house?"

"There used to be other kids but they all moved a long time ago."

Bending down I gave both boys a hug.

"Thank you Mr. Gunn but please don't get killed like my Mom and Dad."

"Johnny don't worry we have guns and we have the Army with us. We'll be back later today."

We all said a prayer with Amy and the boys holding hands with us. Then we mounted up in our trucks and waved good bye. I could tell Johnny and Jimmy were worried by the looks on their faces. As we drove away I called Colonel Turner advising him we were just leaving Tocabaga.

We approached check point one and the Rangers signaled for us to stop and Sergeant Smith said, "Great job finding Captain Sessions. Just wanted to tell you guys that. We have no reports of sniper fire between here and check point four."

"Ok thank you very much Smith, see you later."

We drove away quickly speeding up to 65 mph. We drove through the next two points and in front of the college, sitting in the middle of the road was the Iron Maiden. Captain Riley was standing next to her tank signaling us to stop.

We stopped near her tank and she walked over to the side of the truck where Tommy was riding shot gun. Captain Riley was a good looking woman all right and her one piece tanker suit fit her like a glove. On her hip she wore a shiny stainless steel Colt .45 like General Patton did. I maybe old but I am not dead.

Four Star General George S. Patton was a famous commander who in World War ll started the major use of tanks to sweep over the Nazis in France and Germany. He was famous for always wearing a stainless steel revolver on his hip and his men called him "Old Blood and Guts."

Taking off her helmet showing her short blond hair, she leaned in the window near to Tommy and kissed him on the cheek saying, "Good job yesterday guys. I just wanted to tell you that. Maybe you don't know this but Captain Sessions and I have a thing for each other, so finding him meant a lot to me."

Tommy replied, "Thank you Captain we are relieved Sessions is ok; he's our good friend and brother. How is he doing?"

"I spoke to him early today and he's coming along fine."

All of a sudden we heard a bullet zip over head and then another. Riley yelled, "Better get out of here now; I got to kill some snipers."

She jumped into her tank and we heard the motor start as we sped away. As we were leaving we heard … KABOOM. She fired the big 120 mm cannon, those not driving looked around to see what she was shooting at. We hoped she hit the sniper.

Driving away Tommy said, "No wonder Sessions spent so much time at that tank. Let's call it the 'love tank' now that we know what is going on inside during the night."

We all were laughing our butts off as we pulled up to the house and jumped out. This time we went in the main door. Four men stayed outside on guard covering all four corners of the house. Going room to room Tommy found the ball gloves and toy box. Rahim picked up the heavy toy box and carried it out to the truck. I went to the laundry room, living room, and kitchen but found no bodies, only blood spots on the floor.

I yelled out, "Hey did anyone find the bodies?"

Tommy yelled back, "No bodies are here, let's look outside. You take the back yard Dad we will check the front and sides of the house."

We found no bodies inside or outside. Where are they?

Rahim commented, "Look in the church yard, maybe there is a cemetery there."

"Good idea lets go," Tommy shouted.

There was a small cemetery there and we observed two new graves. You could tell they were fairly new because the dirt piled on top did not have any grass. Someone buried the parents but who? Maybe the kids buried them but how could they to that? I just had that feeling that someone was watching us.

We all stood there and said the Lord's Prayer over their graves. We cobbled up some white fence parts and made two crosses. I took a magic marker and wrote Mr. Evans and Mrs. Evans and the date on the plastic cross. I didn't know their first names.

I commented to the men, "Someone is watching us. Someone buried these bodies and I don't think it was the little boys. Keep a look out for anyone."

I walked over to the Rangers standing at the check point and asked, "Have you guys seen anyone around here."

Sergeant Jones answered, "No we haven't seen

anyone and this whole area was searched a few days ago. Why do you ask?"

"Well we came here to bury the parents of the boys we found yesterday. But they were already buried in the church yard."

"Oh we did that yesterday after you left. They were pretty missed up and we didn't want the kids to come back and see them. We put them in body bags and buried them deep so the coyotes can't dig them up."

"Ok great Sergeant thank you for doing that. I still think you need to keep alert as my sixth sense tells me someone is watching us. We are heading down to the next church and will be back in a few hours."

"See you then Jack."

Arriving at the Blessed Trinity Church there were about sixteen Rangers on guard. Gun Smoke the fighting vehicle was gone. Getting out of the truck we all walked up to Sergeant Major Willis, whom we assumed was in charge, sitting in his Humvee.

As we approached he jumped up and said, "We were expecting you."

"Hello Willis, when was the last time someone was inside the church?"

"We searched that church for men and guns three times yesterday but not today. We have not seen any al-Qaida men around here since we killed a bunch of them yesterday. If you like I can have my men search it again before you go inside but I think it's safe because my men were standing guard all night."

I asked, "Where did Gun Smoke go?"

Willis said, "We heard some shooting down the road so Gun Smoke and eight Rangers went to have a look see."

"That could be a trap or a diversion to draw some men and Gun Smoke away from this church. How long have they been gone?"

Just then we heard the 25 mm chain gun firing in rapid order and other small arms fire about half a mile away. From the sound of it they had found the enemy.

The radio hissed, "We have encountered heavy fire and are engaging the enemy."

SGM Willis replied, "Pull back to the church, do not engage and rejoin us here."

Just then bullets started flying at us. Looking over my shoulder I saw a figure about 300 feet away getting ready to fire an RPG, he was aiming at the Humvee where we were all standing. I quickly raised my rifle and fired two rounds and one hit him for sure but he had already pulled the trigger on the RPG.

The rocket was coming at us like it was in slow motion, I yelled, "RGP hit the dirt."

The RPG round exploded hitting the machine gun mounted on top of the Humvee. It blew the crap out of the gun knocking it completely off the truck. Thank God no one was hurt. AK 47 gun fire was coming from all around us. Our only cover was the Humvee and our two trucks, which are not bullet proof like the Hummer. Since we were more or less in the open the situation was becoming serious. We were all on the ground firing at all sides because bullets seemed to be coming from everywhere.

An AK 47 fires a 7.62 x 39mm round. It is an assault rifle developed in the old Soviet Union by Mikhail Kalashnikov in 1947. Officially it is called the Auto Kalashnikov hence AK 47. It is the weapon of choice for terrorists since it is cheap and readily available. Worldwide more of these guns were produced than any other type. It is a sturdy rifle and dangerous at close range but it is not very accurate.

Tommy yelled, "We got to move inside the church for cover."

Willis replied, "Jack, make a run for the church door one at a time while we provide cover fire."

I got up, ran to the door, pressing the door handle down while bullets were slamming into the big wooden door all around me. I pushed the door but it didn't budge, it was locked.

I thought oh shit now what and I yelled, "The door is locked!"

The sound of gun fire drowned out my yell and I ran back to the cover of the Humvee and yelled again, "The door is locked! Who the hell locked the door?"

Willis looked at me and screamed, "That's impossible, I made sure it was unlocked."

"Sergeant that means al-Qaida is in the building. Where the hell is Gun Smoke?"

Just then Gun Smoke came rolling around the corner and stopped with eight Rangers jumping out and then it started firing the M240 7.62 mm machine gun in all directions.

Willis got on the radio telling the commander, "Blow down the front door of the church."

Turning the turret, taking aim, the 25 mm cannon opened up blowing down the door, and also blew out our ear drums. We all jumped up and ran for the door. Falling inside Ron tripped over a dead body, al-Qaida was inside. He must have been standing at the door when Gun Smoke fired. If there is one fighter there is more.

While the Rangers were fighting outside, we were inside and on our own. We didn't know what to expect. I scanned the room as did Tommy and everyone else. If these men are in the church they must want something here pretty bad. How many of them are here is the question? We huddled together to make a plan.

Tommy pointing to the end of the sanctuary asked Ron, "What's behind those doors?"

"Both doors open into the same big room. There is one door at the back of that room. I don't know where that one goes. Maybe it goes outside."

Tommy stressed here is the plan, "Dad go down the right side and I will go down the left side to the doors in the back of the church. Check all the pews carefully on the way down. Jim Bo, Chris, Rick, Tony, and Ron you cover the doors down there and follow behind us about 10 feet apart, if anyone pops up blast them. Eddy, you and Rahim watch this front door. Any questions?"

Rahim meekly asked, "Hey guys I think I need a gun."

I replied, "You told us you never shot a gun."

"No Jack, I never shot an AR 15 rifle but I have shot hand guns at the gun range many times, so just give me a pistol."

"Do you know how to use a Glock?"

"What is there to know just aim and shoot. Yes I have shot a Glock before."

"Ok fine here's my Glock and 3 mags; just keep your finger off the trigger unless you are aiming at a bad guy. I don't want you shooting any of us. Don't point your gun at anyone unless you are going to shoot them, you got it."

"Yes I got it Jack."

I hate giving a gun to a person who I am not

sure can shoot or even knows the basic rules for safe gun handling. I know people who have shot themselves and others by mistake. Handing a gun is all about training. You drum certain rules into your brain so they become automatic. You don't need to think about it. Practice and more practice is what you need to be a good safe shooter. I would shoot more than 500 rounds per week back in the old days. The two most basic rules are never point your gun at anyone unless you intend to shoot them and never put your finger on the trigger until your target is in your sights.

We proceeded down the right and left sides of the 100 foot long church cathedral hall. At the other end there were two doors one on each side and in the middle was the pulpit with a huge cross hanging on the wall.

I was wondering if someone was hiding behind the pulpit. I kept my eyes on it while looking down the pews. Once we got to the doors, what is behind door one and door two? It sure wasn't going to be a washing machine from Monty Hall. I knew there had to be more al-Qaida fighter's right here inside this church and we have to kill them before they kill us.

Outside I could hear rifle fire and cannon fire from Gun Smoke. They had a battle going on against an unknown number of enemy fighters.

As Tommy and I approached the doors we both looked behind the pulpit, no one was there thank God. Going slowly, ever so slowly we reached our doors. I looked up at the big cross handing on the wall and made the sign of the cross on my chest. I am not Catholic but I do the sign of the cross every time I see one out of respect.

Tommy whispered, "Grenade."

Tommy showed me with hand movements … on the count of three … open the doors and we throw in the hand grenades at the same time. I signaled ok I understand, back to him.

One, two, three … we opened the doors just enough to throw in the grenades. Three seconds later … KABOOM, one second later … KABOOM. Both exploded and if anyone is in there they are dead meat.

We stood there a minute, Jim Bo, Rick, and Tony were behind me; Ron and Chris were behind Tommy who told us, "I will go in first. Dad as soon as I go in you come in. Everyone follow the wall, stay near the wall, and keep it at your back. We will go left and you go right."

We all nodded our heads and Tommy slowly pushed his door wide open expecting gun fire but none came and he entered the room with Ron right behind him. I opened the door and went inside. The room had a few broken chairs and tables and to our surprise two dead fighters were lying in the ruble. We checked them to make sure they were dead even if they were blown to shit. We removed their weapons and unloaded them.

There was one door at the back of the room. Tommy put his ear to the door, I looked thru the key hole, an old trick I remember from when I was a kid. I saw two men standing there in a hall way pointing their guns at the door. I put my finger to my lips to signal, don't make any noise, and waved everyone to move away from the door to huddle together.

I told my guys in a very soft whisper, "I see two men with guns pointed at the door. The minute they hear anything they will fire so stay away from the door. Does anyone have any ideas?"

Tommy whispered, "Let's put the SAWs on the

floor, me on one and Tony on the other, then we'll blast right thru the door killing anyone on the other side."

This was a good idea as the door was wood. I have seen these machine guns blast thru concrete block. The wooden door would be no problem and the two guys behind it would be dead in a second or two.

"Ok let's do it but be quite," I whispered.

Tommy lined the guns up about 40 feet away at the far wall. Tony and Tommy laid down and we all covered our ears as this was going to be loud. They opened fire on full automatic blasting the door to pieces in a few seconds. They fired 100 rounds each or a total of 200 rounds. The firing stopped and they reloaded.

Tommy yelled, "Dad, check the hall way and if anyone is alive shoot them."

Ron and I went and peeked into the hall barely sticking our heads around the broken door jamb to see if any bodies were there. Holding our M 4 carbines we were ready to fire. To our amazement there were no bodies there.

I yelled out, "There all gone, no one is here."

Tommy jumped up and walked over saying, "What do you mean no one is there?"

As Tommy walked into the hall way my phone rang, I answered, "Jack here."

"Jack this is Willis here, we are under heavy fire, there must be 200 fighters here so I called Iron Maiden and some more back up troops. Are you ok? My men in the back of the building heard gun fire coming from inside."

"That gun fire was us shooting at some al-Qaida fighters. We are ok so far but I don't like clearing this church."

"Jack I think the church is surrounded so be careful. These fighters want something in that church for sure."

"Yes I know just keep them out of the church."

"Roger that Jack, over."

Looking down the hallway there were two doors and we didn't know which one the bad guys went in. One metal door was at the end of the hall and it had bullet holes in it from our gun fire. The other door was on the side of the hall. Standing in the hall way we where now the possible targets. They could shoot thru the door, like we did, or throw a hand grenade inside.

I didn't like standing there in the tiny hallway

and told Tony, "Keep your eye on that rear door if anyone opens it, blast it with the SAW."

Ron looking thru the bullet holes in the metal door said, "This door goes outside. I don't see anyone. Should I open it?"

"Ok go ahead but do it slowly. Everyone ready."

We all kneeled down and aimed our guns at the door while Ron turned the handle and said, "It's locked."

"Are you sure it's locked?"

"Yes Jack it is locked try it yourself."

"Ok who is going to open the other door and go in first?

"Just kidding I'll go first, Ron behind me then Tommy, Chris, Jim Bo, and Rick last. Tony you stay here and be the rear guard. First I'm going to throw in a grenade just to be safe. After I throw this in wait 10 seconds and then we enter. Check your weapons and reload them. Is everyone ready?"

I looked at each person in the eye and they all nodded looking me. That told me we were ready. I slowly opened the door about a foot while holding the grenade, pulled the pin tossing it inside, and closed the door.

The blast shook the door but it sounded funny like a hollow explosion in a tunnel. I opened the door and it was very smoky and dark inside, my eyes were slow to adjust and as I was taking my second step forward I fell into a hole about 10 feet deep, landing on my side with a thud on hard cement. I hit my head on landing, almost knocking me out.

I was dazed from hitting my head … wait someone was grabbing me … I had dropped my rifle … I was being dragged by the back of my vest. I reached for my Glock, dam it wasn't there. I was being pulled down a tunnel of some kind. I couldn't fight being dragged backwards and almost knocked out, down a tunnel.

I could hear Ron and Tommy yelling, "Are you ok?"

I was dizzy and couldn't think clearly, what was going on? I got dragged thru a door way, the door closed behind me and I heard it lock. I was in deep shit, this had to be al-Qaida. I pretended to be knocked out so I laid there and didn't move a muscle

They shined a light on my face and I heard a

voice speak in Arabic. I could make out there were two men; one of them kicked me hard in the head. He kicked me in the head again and again, harder each time. Then he bashed me in the face with his rifle butt. That hurt bad and I thought I am going to kill this bastard. My head was spinning I was close to blacking out.

The other person kicked me in the chest. I tried to absorb the kicks without making a sound. He then shined his light on me looking for a gun. I had none and lucky for me he didn't see the knife in my vest probably due to its black handle which was covered by a vest cloth. He saw my ID card on the shiny metal chain and yanked it off my neck. Now they knew who I was and they started to argue with each other.

I could hear Tommy far off in the distance faintly yelling for me. I had gained some time to clear my head. I could move my hands but I broke a couple of fingers on my left hand, good thing I am right handed. I slightly opened my eyes to look and there was a dim light on the ceiling of the room. They were standing at my feet.

I mentally scanned each part of my body for

damage, arms, legs, feet, neck, all seemed to be moveable but my left side hurt like hell. Maybe I broke a couple of ribs. I could function in a fighting mode and knew if I didn't try, it would be the end. I was thinking; I don't want to die in a black hole in the ground at the hands of al-Qaida scum. They still thought I was knocked out.

As they talked to each other I thought I need to make a move now and kill these dorks before they kill me. It was just a matter of time before they would kill me and I am not going to let that happen without a fight. I was trying to physic myself up, getting ready to make the move. I planned the attack in my mind. I have two assholes to kill so I need to be fast and accurate.

I slightly opened my eyes again watching them; both men took off their Arabic head scarves called a Keffiyeh. I thought, *good now I have a clear spot to cut their throats.* I slowly raised my right hand putting it on my knife handle. A tall man had his back to me while taking to the other person whose view of me was blocked.

I pulled my knife out and when it was clear of the scabbard and firmly in my hand, I jumped up as fast as I could while at the same time shoving the 8 inch blade of the double edge Cold Steel knife into his back right below his left shoulder blade, hoping the blade would go in and puncture his lung.

I pushed it in his body with all my strength up to the hand guard. I quickly pulled it out and slashed him across the juggler vein on his neck. He let out a big moan and fell to his knees holding his neck trying to stop the blood from flowing out of his body.

The other shit head went for his AK 47 lying on the ground but I kicked it away from him and it slid about 10 feet. The little shit pulled out a knife and started to quickly slash at me swinging his knife hand back and forth while backing up to the wall yelling something in Arabic. I thought I heard him say my name. He was inching closer and closer to his gun. I had to make a move to stop him.

I decided to press forward thinking I have on two vests; one is my bullet proof vest and on top of that is my combat vest with pockets full of ammo and tools. To stab me in the chest and penetrate the vests would be very hard to do. Looking at his knife it wasn't big enough. I stepped forward he slashed out lunging at me and then I felt his blade pressing on my chest.

I instantly wacked at his knife arm with my Cold Steel Black Bear, all most cutting it off, he screamed as my blade hit his forearm, I heard his bone snap. With a back swing of my blade I sliced his neck wide open and warm blood squirted out at first, spraying all over me, then it began to flow freely from his throat like water.

He grabbed my right wrist to stop my knife but suddenly let go and held his neck to stop the bleeding. I was getting ready to slice him again when the door was kicked in by Tommy and Ron. Tommy promptly shot him in the head. He dropped dead on the spot. The whole thing was over in two minutes but it seemed like it lasted an hour.

The tall dork was on his knees still holding his throat trying to stop the bleeding. Ron had his Glock pointed at his head and was going to shoot him but he said something.

He was bleeding out slowly but surely, he was as good as dead, but managed to ask in a thick Arabic accent, "Are you Jack Gunn?"

Bending down grabbing him by the hair I

twisted his head up so he could see my face and looking closely in his eyes I replied, "Yes I am Jack Gunn."

I let go of his hair then he fell over dead on the cold cement floor, into a puddle of his own warm blood. I pried my ID card out of his dead hand.

I know how to knife fight. I was taught by one of the best a Navy Seal named Mike. He was a knife expert and once told me he killed more men with a knife than a gun. In knife fighting you never hold a knife over hand or over head. You never stab downward but jab and slice. It takes a lot of practice to learn proper knife fighting methods. I also trained with my buddy Russell. Russell was a retired Marine who loved knifes and hand to hand combat.

A good fighting knife has a one piece shank and blade. It is made of hardened steel with a softer inner core but the blade edge is hard and sharp as a razor blade. Fighting knifes have a finger hook or sub hilt for your index finger to wrap around and a hand guard to keep your fingers from getting cut off. The nice thing about the Black Bear Cold Steel knife is that both edges are sharp as a razor so you can slice and dice in either direction.

Tommy yelled, "Wow, are you ok Dad?"

"I am a little banged up, I broke two fingers and maybe some ribs, but I'll be ok. I just need to rest all my energy is gone."

I pulled out my camel back water hose, took a big drink, and asked, "Hey anyone got some booze?"

Rick said, "Here Jack have a drink and he pulled out a water bottle filled with vodka and tossed it to me."

Catching it I mumbled, "Thanks Rick"

I took a big double gulp and then drank some more water. Then I taped my broken fingers together on my left hand. I had on combat gloves but didn't take them off for fear I wouldn't be able to get them back on with swollen broken fingers.

Trying to gain my breath back I felt sick and puked on the floor. My hands were shaking as always after a physical fight and my legs gave out. Falling to the floor I sat down in a pool of warm slippery blood. My strength was gone; my adrenalin was all used up.

Ron asked, "Jack, are you ok?"

"OK, Bro give me a minute to rest."

Tommy came over, shined his light on me, and said, "Dad you're pretty banged up."

"I'll be ok in a few minutes Tommy."

Tommy took out a handkerchief, soaked it in water, and wiped the blood off my head and face for me. That felt really good. I sat there and looked at my vest where the knife stabbed me. Just as I thought it only cut the vest a slight amount. All my men were standing there watching me to make sure I was ok.

I prayed out loud, "Thank you God for giving me the strength to defeat my enemies.

"Hey check these guys out, look in their pockets and see who they are, just don't stand there. I want to know how that ass hole knew my name. They were going to kill me. I need to get glasses. I didn't even see the dam hole."

Jim Bo yelled out, "Bingo look at this! It looks like a wanted poster with your picture. It's written in Arabic but it has above your picture $100,000."

"Jim Bo let me see that. Well that dork knows who killed him. It kind of makes me feel good he found Jack Gunn and went to Never - Never land."

Sure enough Jim Bo was right. I will have to

have Rahim translate it for me. I stuffed it into my pocket, while looking around the room which was about the size of a two car garage, I saw a small 20 x 20 picture of Jesus on the wall and told Ron, "Check if anything is behind that picture."

Ron walked over to it and said, "The picture is screwed to the wall. Hey there is another door here but it is locked, the keys are in the door. I think this is a secret passage that goes to the Priest's house."

"Well take out your Leatherman and unscrew the picture. But be careful it may be rigged to blow up. Keep your eye on that door if anyone opens it shoot them."

After a couple of minutes Ron yelled, "Double Bingo here's a safe."

Tommy walked over to the safe and checked it out saying, "It's not locked; I am going to open it hold your ears just in case it blows up."

Tommy started to laugh as he slowly opened the safe door and we all ducked low as possible and covered or ears. The door opened and there was no explosion.

I yelled to Tommy, "What the hell are you

laughing at!"

"I was just joking Dad but when you see what is inside here you will laugh your ass off."

I managed to crawl to my feet and everyone came over to the safe to see what was inside. There were white money bags inside. Tommy pulled one out and started to dump the contents on the floor. The contents were shiny gold coins along with paper money. It was the loot we were looking for all this time. We all started to laugh. I guess you could say we had the last laugh.

"Dad how much do you think is here?"

"I guess about $500,000 in gold coins and an equal amount in paper money. Let's grab the money and get out of this shit hole now! Tommy keep an eye on that door. I don't want to get surprised by al-Qaida again."

Everyone had a bag of gold coins and paper money as we walked down the tunnel back to the metal ladder to climb out. We made it back to the main church door where Rahim and Eddy were waiting.

Eddy said, "Where have you guys been so long? I tried to radio you but got no reply. What do you have there?"

Tommy told him, "We got the loot Eddy, maybe 1 million dollars."

"Man what a haul. The Rangers wanted to know why you were taking so long. Things are getting hot out there and they brought in more troops and the Iron Maiden. It is also getting dark so we need to leave."

I handed Rahim the paper with my picture and asked, "Rahim can you translate this for me? Oh and give me back my Glock, loaning it to you almost got me killed."

"Sure Jack but you don't look to good. It says … Jack Gunn … wanted dead … for killing our leaders Aamir and Abdul Aalee. Reward for his head is $100,000 in gold coins. This was issued by Osama Hussein the grandson of their Great Leader Osama bin Laden."

"Hey, maybe one of the guys I killed was Osama Hussein grandson of Osama bin Laden. How in the hell did they know I killed Abdul Aalee?"

Rick stuck his head outside the door and a bullet almost blew it off, he yelled, "Things are too hot out there to leave now."

I got on the radio to Willis, "This is Jack we are done here what is the situation out there?"

"Jack, it's not good. Did you find anything?"

"Good news we got the al-Qaida loot and killed five fighters we found inside the church."

"Jack, you guys sit tight for now until we get this mess under control. Both your trucks were destroyed by RPGs. We will take you all back to Tocabaga in a Bradley."

"Ok Willis let us know when we can get out of here."

Rahim came up to me and said, "Jack I know what Osama Hussein looks like. He is the key man for al-Qaida international and that is a big deal."

I asked Tommy, "Can you take Rahim to see the bodies of the two men I killed."

Tommy replied, "Yes let's go Rahim."

Thirty minutes later they came back and Rahim advised me, "The bigger man was Osama Hussein and the other man was his body guard. They were very bad men."

Tommy said, "Look at this I took some pictures of the bodies on my cell phone so we can post them on the internet just to demoralize them."

"That is a good idea," I replied.

I called Colonel Turner on my cell, "Colonel this is Jack, we still at the church and are pinned down for now. I have some good news, we killed Osama Hussein the head al-Qaida leader and found about one million of their cache.

"Colonel, we took some pictures of the dead body and Tommy thinks we should post them on the internet to demoralize them."

"Send them to me and we will do that right away. Sergeant Willis is going to get you back to Tocabaga in a Bradley because it is too dangerous and I understand your trucks were blown up. I have to go now Jack."

"Roger that Colonel."

Sergeant Willis yelled, "Come on guys Gun Smoke is here ready to leave."

We ran out the front door one at a time and jumped into the back of Gun Smoke. I stopped and looked at my smoking burning truck and remembered the kid's toys. I ran to the truck, opened the back, grabbed the undamaged toy box, and darted to Gun

Smoke. I threw myself and the box inside at the same time. Bullets were zipping by me in the air, pinging off the metal sides of the Bradley.

The Bradley Commander Master Sergeant Santelli asked, "Is everyone on board?"

Rick shouted, "Everyone is on, let's go! The big back door began to close."

Gun Smoke moved forward with a big jerk. It was noisy as hell and the sound of the bullets hitting the outside echoed inside making everyone duck. Soon we were out of the hot zone. We arrived back at Tocabaga with no further incidents. I lost all track of time so I looked at my watch it was 8 pm. We were all dead tired and hungry.

Walking over the bridge it felt really good to be in a safe place. The guards all greeted us and asked where our trucks were. Ron told them blown to shit. We took Rick's pickup truck sitting on the side of the bridge where he left it from this morning. We each carried about 10 pounds of gold into my house and dropped it on the floor along with the toy box.

Rick, Eddy, Tony, Ron, Tommy, Rahim, Jim Bo, Chris and I all hugged each other and I told them,

"Great job guys, thank you."

Hemmi came up and gave me a kiss on the cheek and said, "You dummy; you scared the crap out of us. You should have called. Jack you look a mess. Go take a hose shower and wash all that blood off and change your clothes before the kids see you."

"Sorry Honey we had no time to call."

Hemmi handed me a clean pair of pants and a shirt. I ripped off the bloody clothes and Tommy threw them in the dumpster. She held the hose on me and I washed off putting on clean clothes, it felt good.

Amy took the tape and glove off my hand, looking at my fingers she said, "I'll call Doc. Scott right now to set these fingers. It's clear you were in a fight your eyes are swollen and are turning black and blue. You have to go to the Clinic right away."

"Ok I'll go."

Johnny and Jimmy came running downstairs giving everyone there a hug and Johnny said," You got... you got our toy box." He didn't even notice my beat up face.

He opened the lid and found his ball gloves, bat, and ball. Johnny handed Jimmy one glove and they were smiling. It was like a treasure chest, Shanda and Kendra just had to look inside. Johnny invited them to check out the toys.

Rick, Eddy, Rahim, Chris, and Tony left to go home, it had been a long day.

Johnny and Jimmy both yelled, "Thank you Mr. Gunn!"

I softly spoke to them, "My name is Grandpa Jack from now on."

Johnny told me, "We never had a Grandpa."

"You and Jimmy have one now."

Jimmy asked, "Who is going to be our Dad and Mom?"

Tommy said to them, while hugging his wife Tonya, "We'll be your Dad and Mom. Now everyone give a big group hug."

It brought tears to my eyes, after the group hug I went outside, Jim Bo, Ron, and Tommy followed me out; Tommy said, "Dad lets go get a shot of JD at the bar and have a smoke."

"Great idea I have to go see the Doc. anyway."

I yelled to my wife, "Honey we'll be back soon we are going to the bar for a drink and I got to go see the Doc."

We all jumped into my other truck and drove to the bar. Walking in we found the rest of the crew with about 50 people there asking what happen. Rick and Eddy were telling the story as all our friends were shaking our hands and slapping us on the back. I had two shots of JD and went to see the Doc next door, taking the whole bottle of JD with me.

Doc. Scott told me, "Sit down show me your hand."

My fingers were now swollen up twice their normal size. Doc. gave me a shot in each finger to kill the pain. Feeling each finger he pulled them straight while I drank two big gulps of JD. It hurt like hell even with the pain shots. Doc. Scott set my fingers putting on a splint and wrapped them in tape, along with my whole hand. He advised me not to use this hand for about six weeks.

He then looked me over and noticed I had pain in my ribs, feeling them he said, "You have three broken ribs. I'll tape you up."

Then he looked at my face seeing my black and blue eyes and the big bumps on my head he commented, "You may have a concussion. So take it easy for a while. What happened out there?"

"I fell into a pit, got knocked out, lost my gun and two al-Qaida fighters grabbed me, it's a long story but I killed them both with my knife. We found about 1 million dollars that belonged to al-Qaida."

"No shit, Jack you are one crazy dude. Thanks for what you do."

"Thanks Bro., see you later."

I went back to the bar as I walked in everyone came over to shake my hand on killing Osama Hussein. I had two more shots of JD and told Tommy I was going home to rest.

Tomorrow is another day and we will need to weigh the gold and see how much money we obtained and then put it in our bank. I need to review the security situation for Tocabaga. I will ask Tommy and Ron to do an ammo check and gun count.

I have to phone Sessions also to tell him what happen today. I need to talk to Colonel Turner about moving the Muslim women to the Islamic Society in Tampa and the fact we need a chopper to do that.

Work never stops here if you want to stay alive.
I am beat up, in pain and ready to rest for the night.

MAY 17, 2025

I woke up and moaned getting out of bed, my fingers hurt, my back hurt, my ribs hurt, and my head hurt. It was not easy to move my body because of the pain. I went down stairs and took four aspirins, a total of 2,000 milligrams.

My wife Hemmi looked at me and said, "You look like shit Jack."

I replied, "I feel like shit. Give me a shot of whiskey and a cup of coffee."

Sipping on the hot coffee and then downing a shot of whiskey I felt a little better. After a few minutes the aspirin kicked in and I felt better except for my broken fingers. I removed the tape on my fingers and from my chest and took a cold shower to wake me up.

It was cold but it woke me up. I looked at the clock it was 8 am. I never sleep past 6 am and felt I wasted two hours sleeping. I went outside for a smoke and found Tommy and Jim Bo outside. They both said good morning.

Jim Bo asked, "How do you feel?"

"I feel like shit Jim Bo. How do you feel?"

Neither one replied to me as I pulled out a smoke. I was not in a good mood and they knew it. I was in a lot of pain today. The next day the pain is always worse when you have an injury. My head really hurt and I could hardly move my jaw to speak. My whole head felt like someone kicked it a number of times. Oh yes, I remember someone did kick me in the head.

Thinking back I was amazed at what we did. I looked down at the floor while going for a cup of coffee and saw the pile of money on the floor. I felt dizzy and did not feel well at all. I fell down on the floor and couldn't move then everything went black.

Hemmi yelled, "Tommy come and help your Dad!"

I was out of it and don't remember what happened until I woke up a few hours later. Hemmi brought me some food to eat but I just looked at it not wanting to eat. I fell asleep and woke up about eight hours later.

Getting out of bed I didn't know what time it was, looking at my watch it was 5 pm so I went down stairs and everyone was eating dinner. My grand kids, Shanda, Kendra, Johnny and Jimmy came running over to me and gave me a big hug. I gathered them all in my arms as best as I could and hugged them back.

I was feeling better already. Their energy was flowing into me giving me strength. Nothing else mattered at the time. A warm feeling ran through my body, I was being healed, I could feel the energy, it was electric, the feeling of love. What a feeling it was to have these great kids hugging me, I started to cry. Tears ran down my cheeks as I sat there, I was speechless.

I didn't want to let the kids go from my hug because it felt so good but Hemmi asked me, "Jack do you want to eat something?"

"Yes give me some fruit and whatever you have."

I was eating and Johnny asked me, "What happen to your face Grandpa Jack?"

I told him, "I fell into a hole and hit my head and face. I'll be ok."

Then the kids all went to play and I went outside

71

feeling better and thinking about what just happened. I felt better, almost normal, my pain for the most part was gone expect for my broken fingers and ribs. God heals all things if you believe and I do believe in God.

Hemmi asked me, "Jack are you ok now?"

"Yes Honey I feel much better now, so don't worry."

Ron, Jim Bo, and Tommy just looked at me and Tommy said, "Dad go back to bed you need the rest. Don't worry about us we are fine. We weighed and counted the money and there is a grand total of 1.2 million dollars using the current gold price of $11,000 per troy oz. We took it to the bank and it is all locked up and safe."

"Great job, I am going to bed now. I need more rest. I guess I got kicked in the head harder than I thought, good night."

MAY 18, 2025

I woke up at 4 am and actually felt pretty good. I was hungry, needed a cup of coffee. I went down stairs and Tommy was there having a coffee and he poured me one.

We walked outside and he asked me, "How do you feel today?"

"I feel a lot better, almost normal."

"Dad you need to take it easy, slow down, you are not a spring chicken anymore. You take too many risks."

"Yep, you're right but I don't feel old and I am in pretty good shape for an old fart. I took care of those al-Qaida fighters." Deep down I knew Tommy was right.

"Dad, you shouldn't go running or lift weights for at least another week. Let's get something to eat."

We walked into the kitchen and grabbed a few oranges. Soon the girls would be up and would cook some breakfast and I could eat a horse. That's it, I needed some good red meat to help repair the damage done to my body, I needed protein, but we only had chicken meat, eggs, and fish. That would have to do for now.

I sat down at the table to make up a work list. Tommy and Ron need to do a gun count and ammo check. I need to call Colonel Turner about moving the Muslim women to the Islamic Society in Tampa. I also wanted to call Captain Sessions. Rick needs to set up a meeting to discuss how to handle the loot we found.

After I took a shower and ate four eggs, a piece of fried fish, and an apple I gained some energy, so I told Tommy, "Let's walk down to the bridge and see what is going on."

We both put on our bullet proof vests and then our combat vests over top. Putting our hand guns in their holsters we went to the safe to obtain our rifles. I pulled out my Black Bear and saw it had blood on it so I washed it off and cleaned it. Pulling out my sharpening stone I ran it up and down the blade as we walked to the bridge. No wind was blowing so it would be another hot day.

Tommy commented, "Too bad you and Uncle

Ron got your trucks blown up."

"Those were good trucks. Now I only have only one truck which is not trustworthy."

"Tommy what do you think we should do with all the money we found?"

"Well I think Camp Tocabaga owes you and Ron a new truck. They got blown up doing the work of the people."

As we continued to walk Tommy advised me, "Colonel Turner stopped by the house when you were passed out yesterday and he wants you to go to the hospital at SOCOM to get your head scanned.

"He also told us that al-Qaida is pretty much defeated but you can't kill them all. Good news is it should be a long time before they give us any trouble again."

"So that area on the mainland is safe now?"

"You know it is never totally safe."

"My head scanned, I need a new head, but this could be a good time to fly the Muslim women and kids to the Islamic Society in Tampa. You want to go with me?"

"Yup, count me in on a chopper ride. We could

stop in and see Captain Sessions."

I got on the phone to Colonel Turner and he blessed the idea of flying the women and me at the same time. He told me to report to Captain Clark at the Fort by 11 am today. I looked at my watch it was 8 am.

I called Rahim, "Get the woman and kids ready to go. We will leave at 10:30 am and fly them to the Islamic Society so call your buddy over there and tell him we will be there by noon."

"Ok, that is great Jack. I will have them get ready."

"I will pick you up at 10:30 sharp so be on time.

"Tommy find Ron and get your gear ready, the three of us will go with Rahim. Bring 300 rounds of rifle ammo and the normal amount of pistol ammo. Wear full body armor and a camel back for water. You never know what will happen. Oh and bring some power bars to snack on."

We went home to get ready and give our wives the bad news. When you leave Tocabaga you need to be prepped for anything. It is a jungle out there and we have no idea what we will run into at the Islamic Society. I worry that we may encounter some more al-

Qaida.

Just then my phone rang it was Rahim, "Jack I talked to my friend Mihran and he advised us to land in the big parking lot on the south side of the building. He told me once the women and kids are off the chopper to take off right away. As you may know the Army is not well liked and neither are you. Everyone has seen the pictures on the internet of dead Osama Hussein, killed by Jack Gunn. There is still a reward for your head."

"Shit that's not good. I'll wear a flight helmet with a dark shield so no one can see my face."

"Yes that is a good idea but we do not stay on the ground long or we will be killed."

"Can't we fly a white flag?"

"They don't give a crap about a white flag."

"I'll need to discuss this with Captain Clark who will be flying the chopper; he may not go when he hears this. Rahim just get everyone ready to leave."

I phoned Captain Clark, whom I have never had the pleasure of meeting and I told him the situation. He advised me he'd check out the landing site, file a flight path, and alert SOCOM of our ETA. All in all he did not seem so concerned. He told me the chopper is fully armored and they have two M134 mini Gatling guns.

At 10:30 we picked up Rahim, seven Muslim women, and four children. We rode to the Fort in two trucks. The women seemed happy to be going to the Islamic Society in Tampa. Rahim told them his friend Mihran would take care of them. Some of them already knew Mihran.

Arriving at the helicopter area, Captain Clark walked up to my truck and said, "Are you Jack Gunn?"

"Yes I am Jack, nice to meet you Captain."

Getting out of the trucks we did brief introductions and he asked, "How many people are coming?"

"Ron told Clark, "We have a total of 15 people. Four kids and seven women will go to the Islamic Society. After we drop them off Jack needs to go to SOCOM HQ for a brain scan and we also want to visit Captain Sessions at the Clinic."

"My Choppers can only hold fourteen people each. We need two pilots and a crew chief to man the guns. So we need to use two Black Hawks."

"I was a crew Chief on these choppers for 20 years so I can fill in on one chopper if you agree."

"Ok sounds good divide your group, half in each chopper. We will be taking these two here, Chopper 011 and 012, they are the best we have."

Ron walked around each one looking very carefully at whatever they check on the outside of the Black Hawks. He knew what he was looking at but I didn't. Finally he seemed satisfied so he climbed in and checked out the M134 Gatling guns.

Captain Clark asked Ron, "Are you satisfied everything is A-OK?"

"Yes Sir everything checked out A-OK, let's go."

The Black Hawk is armored to withstand hits from 23 mm shells, and its airframe is designed to crush on impact to protect the crew. The pilot and co-pilot have armor plated seats. The helicopter also accommodates door gunners, who provide security for the crew and aircraft using machine guns.

Additional specifications (UH-60L, most recent model):

Maximum Gross Weight: 23,500 pounds

Empty Weight: 11,516 pounds

Maximum Speed: 193 knots / 222 mph

Armament: Two 7.62 mm M134 miniguns

Rotor System: 5 3 feet, 8 inches in diameter

Length: 64 feet, 10 inches

Height: Varies from 13 feet to 17 feet

Range: 352 miles

I split the group up, Rahim and me with three women and two kids. The other group was Ron and Tommy along with four women and two kids.

Captain Clark introduced Lieutenant Boyer, who was his co-pilot, and Captain Keener with Lieutenant Jones. He reviewed the flight plan and had pictures of the Islamic Society showing where we would land. Clark suggested that we land in a football field right across the street as that way both Black Hawks can land at the same time. He also advised we would arrive at least 15 minutes early to throw off any attack they may have planned.

I thought it was a great plan using a different landing area and a different arrival time. Mihran or any other questionable people would not be expecting us to land across the street.

The flight plan was, take off from the Fort, and

fly over the water at an altitude of 3,000 feet. Once over land we would fly at tree top level as it is harder to hit a fast flying chopper which is close to the ground. By the time you hear it and look up it is gone.

We would unload the women as fast as possible with motors still running. Both Black hawks would then fly to SOCOM and drop us off. One would stay to bring us back to Fort Desoto a few hours later.

We climbed into the Black Hawks and fastened our seat belts. I always liked the joke "In case of an emergency bend over as far as you can and kiss your ass good bye." I hate to fly in anything. If God wanted us to fly we would have wings.

The motors started to whine and the blades began to turn slowly at first then speeding up to create a powerful roar. Then suddenly the chopper moved forward and lifted off the ground. I put on a flight helmet which covered my face and I could talk to everyone in both choppers.

Captain Clark advised us, "The ETA is 15 minutes. So everyone be ready."

Flying over the Skyway Bridge we could see it was falling apart due to no maintenance for the last 5 years. Zooming over Tampa Bay we could see a large number of sharks. I counted ten sharks from my side of the chopper.

Flying in a helicopter is very different than an airplane. You fly low and can see everything, but the main difference is the bumpy, noisy ride. You feel like you are part of the machine, the doors are open and the wind is blowing inside. Your whole body pulsates in tune with the craft.

With land approaching the chopper made a fast dive down and we were flying right over the tops of buildings. Then Clark said, "LZ (landing zone) one minute."

Clark put on the air brakes and the chopper stopped in mid air with the nose pointed up and quickly dropped to the ground bouncing on the landing gear. Rahim and I jumped out and helped the women and kids dismount, keeping low to avoid the wind from the blades. Rahim yelled at them in Arabic to run across the street to the Islamic Society.

The other chopper was unloaded and we were ready to go. Clark was applying power to the engines when we heard bullets hit the fuselage. Captain Clark replied, "We are under fire from the small building at 3 o'clock."

As we lifted off he rotated the chopper moving away from the gun fire. The door gunner fired three buzzing bursts from the M134 Gatling gun into the building as we zoomed away. In less than five minutes we landed at SOCOM, the old Mac Dill Air Force base.

As we dismounted the aircraft Captain Clark said, "Thank you for flying Tocabaga Airlines. The Medical Clinic is located in the third building on the left. I will wait here for your return."

"Thanks Captain Clark," I replied.

Finding the Clinic, which was more like a full blown hospital, we located Captain Sessions asleep in his room.

I gently tapped his shoulder and softly said, "Captain Sessions Jack Gunn reporting for duty."

He awoke seeing us there and reached out to shake our hands saying, "It's great to see you guys are still alive. Hello Rahim."

Rahim nodded his head and said, "Nice to see you Captain."

Ron asked, "How are you doing and when can

you get back to work?"

Before Sessions could answer Tommy commented, "Some people do anything for a vacation."

"I just want to thank you guys for the rescue. I will be out of here in a month they put some kind of new cast on my leg and it greatly reduces the healing time using electronic stimulation."

I asked, "Captain, why did you cut out your implant?"

"I cut it out just in case al-Qaida could track it. Maybe they knew about it and maybe not, but I didn't want to take any chances. How about Johnny and Jimmy Evans, they really saved me and I want them to receive a medal."

"I agree with you they need a medal. By the way they are now living with me and Tommy. Tommy is acting Dad and I am Grandpa Jack. They are happy and doing well."

"Jack, that is great news, I was concerned about them, but now I know they are in good hands. Please tell them I said hello.

"I heard from Colonel Turner that you killed Osama Hussein and found the al-Qaida cache. That is really something."

"Thanks Captain I got beat up pretty good. I came here for a brain scan from them kicking me in the head. Oh by the way we dropped off the Muslim women at the Islamic Society.

"Captain that place must be a hot spot for al-Qaida. Don't you think so Rahim?"

"Well it is true the Muslims living there do not have good friends like I do. They have not adjusted to the American way of life. People there just want to live there in peace for the most part following Islam. There are however some very radical men there for sure. I do not know if they are al-Qaida."

Sessions said, "We have checked them out and we leave them alone as long as they leave us alone. Someday however they will have to follow the US Constitution and our laws."

Just then an Orderly came in and said, "We are ready for Jack Gunn."

I told Tommy, Ron, and Rahim, "Stay here with Sessions and I'll be back soon."

After the scan Doctor Cramer told me I had brain damage due to a concussion. He told me take it easy and don't drink alcohol or take aspirin for about 2 weeks. I thought bull shit I don't need a brain scan to tell me that. I went back to see Sessions.

Walking into his room I looked at my watch it was now almost 4 pm and I said, "Well we're going to leave now. I only got a brain concussion. Captain, if we can do anything for you let us know. Captain Clark is waiting to fly us back to Tocabaga so we better get going."

"Thank you all for coming to see me.

"Oh one more thing, Jack I have assigned Sergeant Major Willis and Sergeant Smith as your security team. These Rangers are the best I have. Please use them whenever you leave Tocabaga as I know about the reward for your head. When my Rangers found out what you did they all wanted to be on your security team."

"Shit Captain I don't want any Rangers getting killed protecting me. I can take care of myself."

"Too bad Jack you got them whether you want them or not. We are also giving you two fully armored Humvees with 50 caliber guns to replace the trucks you lost."

Putting all our hands on top of one another and standing in a huddle around the hospital bed we all said, "Rangers Lead the Way!"

Rahim stood there watching us, I wondered what he was thinking, and if he knew why we did that.

It was a short flight back to Fort Desoto and no one spoke on the way back. As a matter of fact I fell asleep even with all the noise. Landing at the Fort we thanked Captain Clark and made our way to the bar for a drink and a smoke. A little brain damage isn't going to stop me from having a shot or two of JD.

We went home to see the kids and wives and I told Hemmi, my wife, the news of my brain scan. I downplayed it of course so she would not worry. I downplayed it to everyone, but the brain damage was serious. A few more kicks in the head could have killed me. I need a few days of rest for sure.

I have to call Colonel Turner and advise him of my brain scan results. Rick needs to call a meeting to vote on what to do with the gold we found. I have a feeling this meeting could become a heated debate due to what is commonly called gold fever.

May 19, 2025

I woke up late at 8 am and grunted getting out of bed as I was still feeling the broken ribs and fingers. I took a shower and went to the kitchen to find the kids eating so I sat down and joined them.

They all said, "Good Morning Grandpa Jack."

"Good Morning kids. What are we eating?"

Hemmi replied, "I have something special for you fried chicken and greens."

"Great, that sounds good!"

Kendra told me, "We played with Johnny and Jimmy's toys yesterday and they showed us how to play catch."

"So is everyone getting along ok?"

My sons' wife Tonya answered, "Yes the children get along fine and don't fight at all."

"Great I don't want any fighting. You are all brothers and sisters. You need to help each other."

I got up after eating and went outside looking

for Tommy, Ron, and Jim Bo. I was surprised to see SFC Smith and SGM Willis standing next to 2 battle ready Humvees.

"Good morning men."

"Good morning Jack," They replied.

"What kind of orders did Sessions give you for my security?"

Willis said, "Jack we're to go with you anytime you leave Tocabaga or follow any order you give us. Let me say Sir for both of us it is an honor to provide your security."

"Thank you both for your concern about my security. If I plan to leave Tocabaga I will contact you by cell phone, correct?"

"Yes Sir that is correct. When we're not with you we will be standing guard at the main bridge waiting any orders from you. We cannot let you leave Tocabaga without us."

"Ok thank you men, I am going down to the bridge now to have a look around. I'll drive one Humvee and Smith drive the other. Willis you are with me."

My phone rang and it was Rick, "Hey Jack how

did the brain scan go?"

"No problems Rick I am cleared for duty and feel pretty good now."

"Anyway that is good news. The meeting time to discuss the gold is at 5 pm at the community fire circle downtown."

"Fine Rick I will see you then."

I planned to take it easy today by reviewing the defensive positions and going to the town meeting on what to do with the gold. Of course the 12 member board will vote on this based on input from any one at the meeting. My idea is to save the gold for future use. The paper money which accounts for $200,000 we could spend for needed items if necessary.

The problem is we don't know what the future currency is going to be so getting rid of the dollars maybe a good idea. The gold however will always be worth more as time goes on. Arriving at the bridge I asked Willis and Smith to be at the meeting for security reasons just in case a fight broke out, and I mean a gun fight.

I saw Tommy, Ron, and Jim Bo at the bridge and walked over to them, "Hey boys what is going on?"

Jim commented, "Not much Jack we were watching the Dolphins here and saw a couple of big logs float by and a bunch of oil drums a little while ago."

"I wonder where they came from."

"They probably came from Tampa where the oil storage docks are located."

Tommy said, "I see you got the Humvees."

"Yes Ron and I will share them. We can all share them."

"Remember the meeting is tonight make sure everyone is there."

"Ok Dad we'll make sure."

"See you guys later I am going to check the rest of the island."

"Willis and Smith you can stay here or come with me just for fun."

Looking across the bridge to the beach on the other side of the channel I noticed that a few drums had washed up on shore. That made me upset that someone over in Tampa was throwing oil drums into the water. I called Sergeant Cain the Drone Master asking him to put up a drone, and find out where these 55 gallon drums where coming from.

During our inspect of the island defensive positions we notice on the east side, the shallow side of the island there were about 100 drums washed up in the shallows. That really made me mad because now we would have to remove them somehow.

By the time we finished our review of Tocabaga and Fort Desoto it was time for the meeting. My two security guards came with me to the meeting and stood in the back ground. About 75 people were in attendance and I surprised by the small turn out.

Rick started the meeting, "I hereby call this meeting to order. We are here for one reason to discuss the al-Qaida money. If anyone has any ideas on what to do with the 1.2 million dollars please raise your hand and state your idea. We have $200,000 in currency and the rest is gold coins."

A voice came from out of the crowd, it was Kane, "Hey Jack, I see you got your own little army there! None of us have Rangers for our security! Are you going to become a Dictator? Oh I forgot you already are one."

Kane sometimes called Captain Kane is an outspoken drunk and who smokes too much pot. He gets drunk, says things, and does things that sometimes make people upset and then trouble starts. But his comments are way out of line today. Few people care for him and most stay away from him because they don't want any trouble. He has been in more than a few fights because of his big mouth.

Kane is about 5' 10" tall at 210 pounds and shaves his head. Kane thinks he is a tough guy. He came here about 15 years ago and has no family on Tocabaga. When Kane is sober he is almost likeable.

Rick yelled out to him, "Kane you are out of order. Keep to the point and state your ideas or shut up."

"Yeah, you all would like to shut me up. My idea is divide up the gold and money evenly to everyone on Tocabaga. That is the only fair thing to do."

"Ok that is one idea but each person would only get around 2,000 bucks in gold and green backs. Are there any other ideas?"

Without raising his hand Kane yelled, "Wait let's vote on my idea now!"

"Kane we are just hearing ideas and input from the group. So you are out of order again.

"Ok anyone else want to speak?"

Maggie who was married Robbie my best friend stood up and suggested, "I think we should use the currency to buy something for the community, like a tractor to help grow more food and save the gold for the future."

Robbie was killed by the Feds and Maggie has been in charge of our farming since she knows more about this than anyone on Tocabaga. Maggie is a beautiful woman who knows how to take care of herself. Since the death of Robbie she was been pretty much alone and hangs around with other women here keeping busy all the time. Sometimes she comes to the bar for a drink with Amy and Captain Riley. Single men try to hit on her but they don't get very far. They know Maggie is a friend of our family and is under our protection. Robbie did not like Kane.

Kane yelled out, "Maggie that is a bullshit idea. We don't need a stinking tractor!"

"Yes we do because most of the farming work we do is all by hand. You don't work the fields so you have no idea how hard it is!"

"So you just want to make it easy work by having a big tractor. I don't think a woman should have any say about the money."

Jim Bo replied, "Shut the hell up jerk, I mean Kane! You are out of line."

I commented, "I think buying a tractor is a great idea because we only have a small one and it's 30 years old. We could also buy some solar generators."

Rick spoke up, "If no further ideas … then all in favor of buying a tractor and solar generators with the currency raise your hands."

I counted 75 votes in favor of the tractor. That is a majority of the votes possible. The Board will vote next and follow what most of the people here voted for. There was no sense in taking a vote for the idea Kane proposed.

Kane shouted out again, "The vote is rigged, this is bull crap. I want my money!"

Rick replied, "That is all the meeting is adjourned, the Board will approve the idea that Maggie and Jack suggested."

Willis and Smith here going back to the Fort for the night, Willis commented, "Hey that guy Kane got a chip on his shoulder. You better watch him Jack and if you need us give me a call. See you tomorrow."

Everyone got up to go home but some went to the bar for a drink, among them was Kane who was already drunk and had smoked some pot by the looks of him. I went to the bar along with Tommy, Rick, Jim Bo, and Ron. Amy came along with Maggie and Riley to the bar. I felt there was going to be trouble.

The men were sitting on one side of the bar and the girls on the other. The women were talking about something. Kane sat down by himself in between us. All he did was sit there and bitch that he wanted his money.

"Kane you are drunk why don't you go home and sleep it off," Tony told him.

I wasn't paying any attention especially to Kane as he was getting me angry and I told him to shut the fuck up.

Then he got my attention when he told Riley, "Come on honey you give it away to all the Rangers so let me have some."

The next thing I knew Kane grabbed Captain Riley off her bar stool and was trying to dance with her but was also grabbing her ass.

Riley fighting him off said, "Let go of me, you jerk!"

She pushed him away but Kane came back and grabbed her again. Tommy, Jim Bo, and Tony stood up and were getting ready to take care of Kane.

I watched as Riley quickly pulled out her shiny stainless steel Colt .45 revolver and smacked him in the head, you could hear the blow and he staggered back a little.

Kane screamed, "You fucking bitch," and lunged toward her.

Suddenly Amy and Maggie jumped up off their bar stools, pulled out their guns and began hitting Kane in the head all at the same time. They pistol whipped him until he fell to the ground knocked out. He was out but they kept hitting him in the face until he was a bloody mess. I was worried that they would kill him.

I yelled to the girls, "All right that's enough he is out!"

They stopped hitting him but Riley gave him one more hard hit that broke his nose, causing blood to flow out all over his face and clothes. She spit on him and kicked him hard. He had it coming for sure.

Tommy and Jim Bo, grabbed Kane by the legs and dragged him outside to the alley way to sleep it off. What Kane did to Captain Riley was very serious. He will have to go on trial for his actions.

We all sat down and had another drink trying to calm the women down as they were pretty hyped up from the adrenaline rush.

Tommy said, "I hope this teaches Kane a lesson."

I told everyone, "Kane never learns his lesson. He has a real problem and we can't help him because he doesn't want help. Don't turn your back on Kane or be alone with him. This is far from being over.

"If Captain Sessions finds out what Kane did … look out he might kill him."

Riley commented, "There is no need for Sessions to find out because he will kill Kane."

Everyone agreed and we all had one more drink and left for the night. On the way out we stopped to check on Kane but to our surprise he was gone.

Tommy said to Jim Bo, "We left him lying right here."

Jim Bo looking at me with a puzzled face commented, "Maybe the coyotes dragged him away but if the coyotes got him there would be more blood on the ground, don't you think Tommy?"

"Yep, there would be more blood. Maybe he woke up and went home. Let's do a quick search around here to make sure."

We checked all over the area within 100 feet and found no sign of Kane. We'll follow up and check his house tomorrow.

As always it was one hell of a day. I don't care for Kane but l hope no harm comes to him, even if he did deserve a beating, I don't want him dead. I will check his house at first light. He will have to go on trial for his actions. The problem is what would the punishment be?

MAY 20, 2025

It was still dark at 5 am the normal time I wake up. Yesterday a lot of tension was created by Kane whom suddenly disappeared after the women beat the hell out of him for improper advances. I need to check his house today see if he is ok. I made a coffee, picked up an apple, and went outside. Tommy and Jim Bo where already up and greeted me with a good morning.

"Hey do you guys want to check on Kane with me?"

Tommy and Jim Bo both shook their heads yes and Tommy said, "We can't let you go by yourself. You don't know what that nut is going to do."

I took a sip of coffee and lit a smoke saying, "Yes he is a nut, but he just disappeared. Let's get ready and go find him."

They left to get their gear, vests, and guns on. I was already set to go. Just then Smith and Willis pulled up and their way to guard duty at the bridge and stopped.

"Good morning Jack," They both said.

"You guys want a cup of java?"

Willis replied, "Sounds great, we heard about the fight with Kane at the bar last night from Captain Riley. She's not anyone to mess with."

I poured them both a cup of mud and replied, "Yes I saw the whole thing and Kane got hammered. We took him outside after the fight to sleep it off and when we left the bar he was gone, just disappeared in thin air. We're going to look for him now."

Smith asked, "Do you need any help? You got to be careful because he is not playing with a full deck."

"Yes I know, I have Tommy and Jim Bo coming with me just in case."

Finishing their coffee Smith and Willis said, "Thanks for the coffee Jack and if you need us call."

"Ok guys see you all later."

Jim Bo and Tommy came out and we jumped into the new Humvee and took off to Kane's' house. I was driving as we pulled up to his place about 5 minutes away, on the other end of the island.

I knocked on his door with Tommy and Jim standing next to me, no one answered. I noticed his car was not in the drive way. I turned the door handle and the house was unlocked so we walked in and I yelled, "Kane ... Kane you in here?"

No reply was heard so we searched all four rooms. The place was a mess it looked like someone had ransacked it. I knew Kane was a clean freak and he kept his home spotless. Something was wrong for sure.

Tommy asked, "Now what, he's not here?"

I pulled out the security radio and advised, "If anyone sees Kane let me know."

"Now what? I suggest we form a search team and cover the whole island. We will need about fifty men. We need to look in each house not occupied and each car. We have to check the two lakes and wooded areas."

Jim Bo standing there looking pissed off commented, "That will take days, maybe weeks to do. He's around so let's just wait a few days for him to show up, rather than waste our time."

"Jim you have a good point but let's drive around the island one time and see if we can find him."

"Ok let's go," Tommy replied.

We drove around the island looking everywhere

but couldn't find Kane so we drove back to the bridge. Parking the Humvee we dismounted and walked up to the apex of the bridge. It was now about noon.

Willis asked, "Did you find Kane?"

"Nope didn't find him," I replied.

Ron pointing in the air said, "Look at the vultures circling over there. That means something is dead or dying. It looks like they are flying over by Shell Key."

We all turned and looked up at the vultures; there must have been a fifty of them. That meant something big was dead, so I said, "Ok let's go see what's over there. We didn't search that area."

Ron agreed, "I'll go with you it's lunch time anyway and we can grab some food from the bar."

Arriving on the peninsula behind the old restaurant called Billy's, Chris was on guard duty for that area and as we pulled up he asked, "What's up?"

I told Chris, "Look, see those buzzers flying over head. Something is dead out here.

"Who was on duty last night?"

"Eddy was but no one was here when I came at 7am."

This area is completely over grown with bushes, weeds, and high grass so we all started to look around. Ron found a trail where the grass had been stepped on and pushed down so we followed it. Walking ever so slowly through the high grass, our guns at the ready, we followed the trail to a tree.

Coming to a Palmetto tree we found two bodies lying there tied to the tree. One was Kane and the other was Eddy. Someone had cut their throats.

Crows were already pecking at their eyes and throats but flew away when we arrived. Looking closer the bodies were covered with flies and fire ants having a feast. Nasty little fire ants will eat you dead or alive.

Eddy the beer maker, the pot grower, my trustworthy loyal friend for almost twenty years was dead. We had been through a lot together. Whoever did this to Eddy will pay, an eye for an eye is my code. I will keep my word.

I stood there looking at the bloody bodies, made the sign of the cross and said, "Well guys it's pretty clear what they died from but who the hell killed them?"

We all looked at each other and no one made a

comment. I thought maybe Captain Riley or a Ranger killed Kane but they wouldn't kill Eddy. I had no good ideas. What do we do now?

"Hey, look here is an Arabic head scarf," Tommy advised us, picking it up off the ground out of the weeds.

I thought … shit … al-Qaida is here. They have somehow managed to get on the island.

I pulled out my radio, "Attention all security we have al-Qaida fighters somewhere on Tocabaga. Keep a sharp eye, shoot first, and ask questions later. We are on full alert."

I thought about this and told everyone my conclusion, "This is al-Qaida work. They're here to get my head and collect the reward of $100,000 in gold coins. There must be at least two of them to kill our men like this and I know how they got here."

Ron asked, "How did they get past our security?"

"That's easy they came in those oil drums that have been washing up and floating by."

I phoned Cain the Drone Master and asked him, "Sergeant did you ever find out where the drums were coming from?"

"I was just going to call you about that. The drums are being put in the water in Tampa at the old oil storage area. Based on Drone pictures it looks like the guys doing it are al-Qaida."

"Ok thanks for the information."

"Men, Cain just confirmed the oil drums are being put in the water by al-Qaida. We need to shoot the shit out of each drum. Sink them and fill them full of holes in case someone is hiding in them. I want every drum to look like Swiss cheese.

"Tommy take the east side of the island and Jim Bo take the west. Ron and I will check at each bridge. We will meet at the main bridge in 3 hours. First let's put Eddy and Kane into body bags and get them out of the heat so no more ants or birds eat them.

"We'll have a funeral service later after we kill the men who did this."

I have a plan to locate and kill the fighters that are already here. I'll be the bait. They are here for me so I need to let them find me. I will tell Tommy and the others the full details of my plan later. We need to kill these bad guys today.

Then I thought maybe they know where I live so I called SGM Willis telling him, "Willis go to my house with Smith and guard it because al-Qaida is here on Tocabaga."

"Al-Qaida here on Tocabaga, how is that possible? How many are here?"

"We don't know how many are here but we found Eddy and Kane dead their throats were cut and we found an Arabic al-Qaida style head scarf. I think they came here in those oil drums we have seen floating around.

"By the way have the guards at the main bridge shoot holes in all the drums that have washed up or are floating around."

"Ok Roger that Jack. We will get over to your house ASAP."

My cell rang, it was my wife, "Jack, Johnny was outside and he came running inside telling me he saw a man with a towel on his head. Johnny is scared ... you better come home right away."

"Listen to me Willis and Smith are coming over

right now and I will be there in five minutes. Stay inside, lock the doors, and keep your gun handy. Have everyone keep their guns handy, Bye"

"Ron lets go to the house Johnny saw a towel head outside while he was playing. Everyone is inside now but we need to check it out."

"Let's go Bro."

Willis and Smith were all ready there when we arrived at the house; I jumped out of the Humvee and asked, "Did you guys see anyone?"

"No we haven't seen anyone," Smith replied.

I yelled, "I am home," and ran inside to find Johnny.

Everyone was sitting in the living room with all the shutters closed.

"Johnny, where did you see the men with towels on their heads?"

"I saw them by the bushes near the water. I only saw their heads. They didn't see me."

"Good boy Johnny, don't worry we're all safe."

I radioed Tommy and told him, "You and Jim Bo come to the house when you're finished. Johnny saw a fighter in the bushes here. I have a plan to get these guys."

"Ok see you in about an hour."

I got on the phone to the Drone Master, "Cain this is Gunn I need you to put a drone up watching the Bayway from my house to the bar. If possible put up two drones. We have some al-Qaida guys here and we have to find them quickly. They have already killed two of our men."

"Ok Jack, you got it; the drones will be over head in a few minutes. I will call you when we see them and give you their location."

My Plan was to use myself as bait. I would go to the bar and pretend to get drunk and stumble home in the street by myself. Tommy, Jim Bo, Tony, Ron, Rick, and Chris would be my back up snipers. They would be located 300 feet apart going down the main road with the exception of Tommy who would follow behind me out of site covering my back.

I knew the fighters were watching me, waiting for a chance to kill me. I could feel it, my sixth sense was strong. As soon as it was dark I would walk to the bar. I got ready checking and double checking my guns and gear.

I would carry my trusty Colt CAR 15 9 mm carbine with a 20 round magazine and 4x low light scope. As always I pack my Glock 17 and Cold Steel Black Bear fighting knife. As an added protection I also carried a Glock 19 with a laser sight. I wanted a back up hand gun just in case something went wrong. My sixth sense told me to bring this gun because it had a laser which is very useful in the dark. All you do is just put the red dot laser on the target and fire, you can't miss.

I told my plan to the assembled group and Tommy looking in my eyes said, "Dad don't do this it's too dangerous. We'll get them somehow."

"I need to do this because they want me and the longer we wait more people could be killed. No one is safe on Tocabaga. So it's a done deal. I got you, the best shooter, to back me up, so I am not worried."

Deep down inside I was worried because anything could go wrong.

"Ok everyone get in your positions now. Remember you guys are also covering each other as well as me. When it's dusk I will go to the bar and I will leave there at 10:30 pm sharp. I am counting on everyone to kill these dorks.

"Remember I am going to stumble down the road like I am drunk and I will fall down a few times and lay there hoping the jerks attack me then. I want them to think I'm passed out drunk, being the cowards they are, that's when they'll attack me."

It was 8 pm and the sun was setting. I told my wife and family not to worry I will be home by mid night. I left the house telling Smith and Willis to keep their guard up. They knew my plan and wished me good luck.

It was only a half mile away but it was a long walk. I took my time staying on the east side of the divided highway, paying attention to every detail. Thinking if I were an al-Qaida fighter where would I hide to kill Jack Gunn.

They would need to kill me and cut off my head. They would have to do it in a place that was dark with a lot of cover. Maybe they have a rifle or pistol with a silencer on it so a shot could not be heard. Yes that's it they will use a gun with a silencer to kill me and then drag me into the bushes and cut off my head.

My cell phone rang, answering I said, "Gunn here, what's up?"

"This is Willis. We saw two men following you down the road they are off in the bushes on the west side of the road, about 300 feet behind you."

"Thanks Willis they took the bait so far. If they come back toward you kill the bastards, Bye."

I got on the radio to my sniper team, "Willis saw two men following me to the bar on the west side of the road about 300 feet behind me. They were sneaking threw the bushes. If anyone can get a shot at them take it, but don't miss either of them."

Everyone replied, "Roger that Jack."

I phoned Cain, "Hey Drone Master can you see two men on the west side of the road sneaking in the bushes?"

"Yes Jack we got them on screen. What do you want me to do?"

"Just follow them and keep me posted as to their location. Let me know when they are within 100 feet of me."

"Yes Sir I will follow them like a hawk."

"I am going to the bar and will leave there at

10:30 pretending to be drunk. I am the bait they are after me, so don't let me down."

"Roger that Jack, don't worry."

The problem was my men were all on the east side of the divided highway so it would be hard to get a clear shot. The once manicured lawns and bushes were now an over grown jungle. In the old days you would hear lawn mowers everyday trying to keep the jungle at bay.

The road, officially named Bayway South, is a divided four lane state road with a large center strip or median. There are all kinds of plants and bushes growing wild due to neglect over the last few years. It is all most impossible to see from one side of the road to the other. The Bayway is lined with townhomes and condos on each side of the road most of which are empty now.

I finally arrived at the bar and there were three Rangers there along with Captain Riley to my surprise. I advised them what was going on and they watched the two bar doors in case the fighters decided to come in shooting.

Two hours went by and it was 10:30 time to

leave so I radioed my team, "I am coming out now."

Captain Riley and the three Rangers watched me leave and wished me good luck. I did have two shots of JD to take the edge off. Walking out the main door I fell down the last step landing on my knees and slowly got up.

I headed for the east side of the road knowing Tommy was down the road about 200 feet away. To judge distance we use the light poles which are 100 feet apart. My men are hopefully out of sight and ready to kill these scum bags.

I walked close to the curb, as far away from the median as I could get. My thinking is they would hide in the over grown bushes and attack me at one of the U turn locations.

I called Cain, "Where are the bad guys at now?"

"They are at the Sterling Condo hiding behind a wall near the sidewalk."

"Cain stay on the line with me from now on, let me know when and where they move."

I got on the radio and told my team where the fighters were at. I was walking on the east side of the road parallel to the Sterling; I faked a stumble and fell to the ground. I laid there for a minute, got up, and started to walk again, weaving like a drunk.

Cain spoke, "Jack they are now moving north on the west side and ... wait ... they are crossing the road to the median. They are now at the next U Turn hiding in the bushes right near the road. Be careful they ... are ... pointing a gun at you right now, it's a hand gun of some kind.

"Jack you are within 75 feet of them watch out!"

I heard a slight ... POP ... POP ... POP ... it was a hand gun with a silencer. I felt three bullets hit me and I fell down in the grass. I thought shit I am hit. I heard them running toward me and I turned my head to see them. I could see both of them coming up fast to finish killing me; one had a big ass machete in his hand.

I pulled my Glock 19 out with the laser sight getting ready to fire and then I heard ... BAM ... the unmistakable sound of a .308 rifle. Tommy had shot the one jerk and he fell 20 feet away from me. I carefully aimed the Glock 19 putting the red laser dot on his head and squeezed the trigger. My 9 mm hollow point round blew a big hole in the side of his head, he was dead.

The other dork began to run north trying to get away but he ran right to Ricks' location. I heard a burst of automatic gun fire from an M 4 carbine. The fighter dropped in the road about 150 feet away. I saw Tony run out of the bushes and shoot him in the head. Just like the "Walking Dead" you need to shoot Zombies in the head to make sure they don't wake up from Never - Never land.

Tommy ran up to me and asked, "Dad are you hit?"

"Yes, but I don't know how serious."

I just laid there and didn't move trying to feel if a bullet got past my bullet proof vest. Sometimes when you are hit by a bullet you don't feel it right away. Tommy bent down shinning his flash light on me.

Tommy said, "Dad your left arm is bleeding a lot. Sit up I'll put a tourniquet on your arm and take you to Doc. Scott."

When I looked at the blood and the hole in my arm it started to hurt. It felt like I got punched in the arm with an ice pick. I needed a shot of Jack Daniels.

Tommy and Ron took me to the Clinic and Doc. Scott removed a .22 caliber hollow point bullet from my left shoulder where it hit the bone. The little bullet did a lot of damage but it could have been a lot worst if it was a 7.62 round or a .45 caliber round. Those big rounds can blow your arm off. If the fighter had been a better shooter he could have shot me in the head in which case I would not be writing this, but I was lucky or God was watching over me. In any case it was a close call.

Doc. Scott gave me a shot of something to kill the pain and he dug out the bullet and told me, "You'll lose use of this arm for a few weeks. Your bone is fractured but not fully broken. Keep it in a sling as much as possible but don't baby it, try to move your arm every day. You have a lot of muscle damage. Here is some pain killer."

He handed me some kind of pain pills.

Arriving home around midnight my wife was not happy about me getting shot. Lying in bed I thought how many more fighters are going to come to try and kill me. Are there any more on Tocagaba in hiding? We will need regular Drone patrols to watch for any fighters for the next week.

I need guards posted 24-7 to protect my family. Smith and Willis can stand guard during the day. Tommy, Ron, Jim Bo, and I will take turns guarding at night for the next week. Someone must be watching the children at all times.

How can we stop this? Then it occurred to me. Post it on the internet; post a picture of me dead, killed by al-Qaida fighters who were also killed during the raid. Yes that is the answer to stop these attacks. I will phone Colonel Turner in the morning and ask him to post it on the net.

JUNE 11, 2025

THREE WEEKS LATER

Colonel Turner had my picture taken showing my dead body complete with bullet holes in my head and fake blood. He had it posted on the Net and now we just need to wait and see what happens.

We have not found any more fighters on Tocabaga but the Drones will keep flying just in case for another few weeks, until we are sure the news of my death gets out. The Rangers have killed off and eliminated al-Qaida in our area and for now we are safe. If it wasn't for the Rangers the al-Qaida Army may have taken over Tocabaga. Life is more or less returning back to normal. Our people are back to doing normal everyday tasks of farming, fishing, just trying to live a normal life.

My arm is healing well and I can move it but it is a little stiff. The main thing I am concerned about is getting an infection so I need to keep the wound clean.

My broken fingers are healing well but I have lost some movement. My ribs still hurt but only when I laugh and I now have bad headaches almost every day.

Our Tocabaga security team is back to doing most of the guard details. The Rangers are flying out all the time on patrol up and down the west coast of Florida. Rumor is that the Special Forces along with the Marines have moved on Washington DC and there is fighting taking place. The Marines have orders not to use cannons or bombs in the Capital area, to protect the national monuments from any damage, if at all possible.

The other day Colonel Turner had a medal ceremony, giving Johnny and Jimmy the Army Ranger Challenge Coin, which are only given to someone who has performed a superior act of merit. They also received a framed letter making them honorary Army Rangers. Everyone on Tocabaga was there as well as over one hundred Rangers. Captain Sessions flew in for the ceremony and I am pleased to say he is walking already. He was discharged from the clinic, but is not cleared for active duty. Afterward there was a celebration and the Rangers supplied hot dogs for the whole group. We haven't had real hot dog in years, they were great.

The Army gave us 400 solar generators to use so there is no need to purchase them. They are small and only generate 1 KW but it is enough to run the refrigerator, lights and microwave oven. We hooked them up to each house that is occupied.

Four days ago our little dog Blackie got killed by a rattle snake while playing with the kids. Shanda and Kendra told us that Blackie saved them from the snake by biting it in the head. We dug a hole and buried the brave little dog. I will miss Blackie; the whole family will miss her.

Hemmi, my wife, heard the kids scream, and ran outside with her Ruger .22 shooting the snake ten times. It was a big six foot long diamond back which are hard to kill. I am thankful no one was bit by that big monster.

Maggie found a John Deere tractor for sale on the internet. I don't know anything about tractors but she does and advised me it comes with a tiller, loader, and mower, which is perfect because we can also cut down the weeds and grass. The farmer selling it is just over the Skyway Bridge in Ellenton about 45 miles away. He claims he has other equipment he will sell cheap.

Maggie is pushing for me to go and buy the tractor and asked me, "Jack can we go tomorrow and check out the tractor? It is the only one I found that is close to Tocabaga. I want to come along and get off the island for a day."

"Maggie ok I'll make a plan where is this tractor located?"

"It is at a farm off Route 301 about 5 miles past the old Ellenton Outlet Mall, about 50 miles away."

"Ok Maggie I'll put together a team. It is still dangerous in the outside world so this is not going to be a Sunday drive out in the countryside."

We haven't been across the Skyway Bridge in years. The Rangers now guard it and limit travel coming to this area. No one comes across the bridge unless you have a good reason. The word is that Ellenton area is not safe.

My thinking was we would need the two Hummers, two big pickup trucks and 16 people for security reasons. There would be four people in each vehicle. The convoy would have one Humvee in the lead and one at the rear. We have two F 350 trucks to use for towing.

I plan to take Rangers Willis and Smith, for my security. I need my trustworthy team of Ron, Tommy, Jim Bo, Chris, Rick and Tony. I would bring Maggie and Amy as they are both good shooters and they would ride in one of the Humvees for added protection. Amy would come along to keep Maggie company. I still needed five more men who can shoot.

I called Colonel Turner, "Colonel we are going over the Skyway to buy a tractor to enable us to produce more food. I want to have 16 men go on this expedition but I am five men short. Can you assign me five Rangers to go along for security?"

"Are you taking Willis and Smith along?"

"Yes of course but I am still five short. I need five good shooters."

"Ok I'll tell Willis to select five Rangers to go for added security."

"Great, thank you Colonel, we will leave tomorrow at sunrise."

We spent the rest of the day packing guns and gear and checking the trucks. SGM Willis selected five good Rangers to ride along for security.

I was a little worried about what we would find and I didn't like the idea of Maggie and Amy coming along. If and when the shooting starts you have enough problems trying to stay alive let alone watching out for someone else. Needless to say my wife was not happy about the trip.

JUNE 12, 2025

At 7 am everyone was there ready to go. Willis and Smith were standing there and each had an MK 153 SMAW rocket launcher.

The MK153 SMAW means Shoulder-launched, Muti-purpose Assault Weapon. This is a hand held shoulder fired missile system used to blow up vehicles and buildings. A very powerful weapon that is reusable. You fire a missile and put in a new one.

I gave Willis a curious look and he commented, "We are bringing these little babies along for just in case."

Everyone had a big laugh from that comment and I shouted, "Mount up."

As we drove off of Tocabaga riding in the first Hummer was SGM (Sergeant Major) Willis, two new Rangers who were picked by Willis for security, SPC

(Specialist) Jones and SFC (Sergeant First Class) Kang. Willis drove and I rode shotgun. SPC Jones was in charge of the big gun. The two trucks had one Ranger in each and there was one Ranger in the rear Humvee along with Amy, Maggie, and SGT Smith.

Captain Riley was standing on top of her tank the Iron Maiden as we were leaving and shouted, "Good luck guys!"

Arriving at the toll booth at the Skyway we stopped at a Ranger check point. There were about 12 men there and we told them we would be back today in a few hours. We advised them of our plan because if anything happened this would be the team that would come to help us. Pulling away, Willis hit the gas and got us up to a cruising speed of 55 mph, in ten minutes we arrived at the last check point, the south toll booth. We stopped and informed the Rangers where we were going.

Driving south on Route 75 we arrived at the State Route 301 exit, as we turned off the road it was blocked by two Manatee Sheriffs cars. There were eight Deputies standing in the road. They pointed their rifles at us. We stopped but did not get out and waited for a

Deputy to walk up to us.

Walking up to Willis he asked, "What is the Army doing here?"

Willis advised him, "We are on a mission to purchase a tractor at a farm located on Route 301."

"You need a 50 caliber machine gun to buy a tractor? It sounds to me like you're going to steal one instead. What's the name of the farm?"

"It's Horn and Sons Farm."

"We know that farm it is about five miles east of here. I must warn you that farm is a fortress and has about thirty people living there all armed. They're not friendly and don't like people coming around. They are kind of weird if you ask me. So you need to be careful. Maybe it's a good thing you have some big machine guns."

"Thank you for the warning but they are expecting us. We will be back here in a few hours."

"You guys are well armed so maybe you won't have any problems. By the way where are you guys based?"

"We are based at Fort Desoto, see you later."
The Deputy waved us pass their check point.

As we passed by the old Ellenton Mall we noticed a lot of people hanging around. People were walking around and others were selling junk, guns, or anything to make money on the side of the road. We slowed down but didn't stop and as we drove by many people waved and yelled go Army. Almost everyone carried some type of firearm.

I told Willis, "It looks like a lot of people are living at the mall and this is also a hot spot for buying, trading, and selling goods."

"Yes Sir that is exactly what they are doing. They are trying to stay alive by keeping in groups, the poor fools."

Ten minutes later, Willis stopped the Humvee saying, "Here we are, Horn and Sons Farm."

Looking up there was an old beat up sign hanging that read "Horn & Sons Farm," it was barely readable. It was kind of scary looking with some kind of skulls mounted on each side of the sign. We proceeded onto the bumpy dirt road, the main driveway.

This was a long drive way and we couldn't see any farm buildings. We followed the road for about two miles winding thru old mossy oak trees. I felt like we were being watched. It reminded me of the old movie "The Hills Have Eyes" a story about an inbred family who were overdosed by radiation. They killed people and ate them.

Willis asked me, "What the hell is that smell? It smells like some kind of shit."

"That my friend is the smell of good old pig shit. This must be a pig farm."

The smell was over whelming and even made me gag, so I wondered how Amy and Maggie liked it.

All of a sudden there was a steel gate with ten men standing there pointing guns at us. Looking to my left and right I saw at least another ten men. Most of them had long beards and wore straw hats to keep the sun off their heads. On the other side of the gate about 500 feet away was an old house in need of paint and a barn to the left. I saw a few tractors by the barn. Far to the right I saw the pigs about 300 yards away. The whole compound was ringed by a 12 foot high barb wire fence.

A man walked up to the Hummer and asked, "What you Army boys want?"

I replied, "We're here to buy one of your

tractors. We contacted you by the internet."

"Oh yep, did Maggie come with you?"

"Yes she did."

"Did y' all bring the money?"

"Yes we have the money."

"Good let me see it."

I unzipped the money bag and showed him. He commented, "That's a lot of bucks there. Come on in."

He swung open the gate for us to pull in and Willis got on the radio and told the convoy, "We are going in everyone else stay here outside the gate and be ready for anything. Smith bring Maggie up here and drop her off."

Smith pulled up and Maggie got out. I told her to get in my Humvee. She squeezed inside and we drove into the barn yard where they signaled us to stop in front of a gigantic man. He looked to be about 6 foot 8 inches and probably tipped the scale at 400 pounds.

As we were getting out of the Humvee the large man came over and said, "I am Mr. Horn and these are my boys and brothers. This must be Maggie."

I put out my hand and said, "I am Jack Gunn."

He replied, "I don't give a shit who y'all are."

He walked past me, stepped over to Maggie taking off his hat, and stuck his hand out for her to shake. I didn't want to shake that pig shit hand anyway but Maggie did and afterward I saw her wipe her hand off on her jeans.

I could tell we were going to have problems buying a tractor.

Most of the good old farmer boys came over and just stared at Maggie like she was the first woman they had ever seen, or like she was a fine piece of meat, or a new car. I think they were drooling. I thought we are in trouble for sure.

Horn told his men, "See I told you she'd be pretty."

One replied, "Yes Sir Daddy, she's a looker all right."

"Now back up and give her some room," Horn commanded.

Horn asked Maggie, "How's a pretty thing like y'all know so much about tractors?"

"I studied tractors on the internet and have driven a few. I am a farmer," Maggie replied, looking at him like he was crazy.

"You're a farmer are you? I think you'd be better off making babies." All the good old boys laughed at his comment.

I was thinking Mr. Horn is nuts and these people are weird. I just want to do business and get out of here. I whispered that to Willis and he shook his head yes.

I said, "Mr. Horn can you show us the tractor and equipment?"

"Oh … the tractor … I plum forgot about it looking at this pretty lady."

"Y'all see 'em over there next to the barn and there is some in the barn. Go look at 'em."

I told Maggie, "Come on lets go check them out."

Horn blurted out, "No need for her to go she can stay here with me. The pig shit smell is bad over there."

"I have to go look Mr. Horn, Jack doesn't know anything about tractors," Maggie replied.

Maggie and I walked over to the tractors and looked in disbelief at what we saw. The tractors were all rusted pieces of junk. Each one had tires missing and one didn't even have a motor. They were all totally unusable.

I turned around to see Horn talking to a bunch of his men. I thought oh no we are in deep pig shit now. I saw Willis walk back to the Humvee and open the door. Willis waved at me to return to the Humvee.

I told Maggie, "These tractors are all junk. Let's get out of here these guys are dangerous."

Maggie not sensing danger, shouted to Horn, "These tractors are all junk and don't look anything like the pictures you sent me! Why did you lie about the tractors?"

We briskly walked back toward the Humvee passing close by Horn and his men who were more or less blocking our way when Horn yelled, "Grab 'em boys, get that girl we need another Breeder."

His men grabbed Maggie and one guy hit me in the back knocking me down so I reached for my Glock. Two humongous dirt bags picked me up and took my gun out of my hand like it was a toy. Mr. Horn now had a firm grip on Maggie's left arm, with his huge hand.

Maggie screamed, "Let me go you stinking pig!"

Horn while laughing shouted to Willis, "Hey Army boy throw me the money and I'll let this man go.

But I am keeping this pretty thing to be my next wife. Hurry up now, I have 50 guns pointed at you from that house."

Willis replied, "Fifty guns, thanks for telling me," as he pulled out the MK 153 SMAW rocket launcher and took aim.

Horn yelled, "Hey what the hell you doing?"

It was too late Willis fired the rocket, it zoomed past us making a loud jet roar, and flew into the house …KABOOM … blowing it to shit. Whoever was inside was dead now. The explosion knocked some of the men down, showering us with fragments of wood and glass.

Willis reloaded the launcher and fired it again at the barn … KABOOM … another big explosion.

Jones started to fire the 50 caliber big gun cutting down Horn's men who were all around us. The other Hummer pulled up fast and also opened fire on the nitwits. Dam those big guns make a lot of noise. I was sure glad the Rangers knew how to shot straight since we were in the line of fire. My remaining men jumped out of the vehicles and were all firing their M 4 carbines at the straw hat scum bags.

The big guy that hit me was standing there

frozen from all the noise, the fool let go of me to hold his ears, he didn't like the noise, he was confused and didn't know what to do. I quickly pulled out my Cold Steel knife and stabbed him in the heart; he let out a big roar like a bear being killed. Then I cut his throat, he dropped on the spot.

The other enormous shit head standing next to me reached out to grab my knife so I slashed his fingers off and jumped at him at the same time, stabbing him in the neck. He fell like a big tree trying to hold his head on. I saw my Glock on the ground near his foot, picking it up I shot three other men standing near me before they knew what had happen.

I turned to take aim at Horn who still had Maggie in his grasp; he was dragging her away towards a small building. She was kicking and flailing her free right hand at Horn. I couldn't get a clear shot and yelled to her, "Shoot him Maggie, shoot him!"

Maggie must have heard me yell; using her free right hand she managed to pull out her .38 revolver. She pointed the barrel at Horns' head, a large target you cannot miss, and pulled the trigger, shooting him in the eye, blowing the back of his fat head off. His big obese

THOMAS H. WARD

body fell like a rock, hitting the ground with a thud.

Horn either didn't see her gun or didn't think she would use it. In any case I knew she would without any remorse. Mr. Horn messed with the wrong Breeder.

I yelled, "Come on Maggie run!"

Maggie and I ran for the cover of the Humvee, and jumped inside.

A few moments later the firing stopped. All was quite except for the moaning of the scum bags wounded or dying. There is no telling how many men we killed and we weren't going stick around to find out.

I told Willis, "Let's get out of this pig shit hole and go home."

We sped away down the two mile dirt driveway to Route 301 the main highway. We pulled over there to check if everyone was ok and to see if any damage was done to the trucks. Thank God no one was shot. There were a lot bullet marks on the Hummers and some holes in the pickup trucks but no major damage.

Amy came up to Maggie, hugged her, and said, "That was a close one. Are you ok Maggie?"

"I am ok now that farmer Horn is dead. What a dumb bastard!"

I said, "So much for searching on internet for tractors. Horn wanted you for Breeding. Are you a good Breeder Maggie?" Everyone got a laugh out of that comment.

"Well if everyone is ok let's go home, I had enough for one day."

As we approached the Ellenton Mall, where all the people were hanging out we saw four black SUVs' blocking the road. We stopped a few hundred yards away to see what they were doing.

Willis commented, "They look like Feds to me. They're the only ones that drive those black SUVs'."

Looking threw my rifle scope I saw eight men randomly taking money and guns from the people on the side of the road. On their vests were the letters FBI and ATF. I thought oh no more Feds.

"You are right Willis they are Feds. We can't turn around because this is the only safe way back to Tocabaga."

I told everyone on the radio, "We will pull up and stop to check this out but we will not let them take our guns or money. Everyone be ready."

Pulling up to them, all eight men walked up to

our convoy and circled our trucks. Their guns, H&K UMPs' were at the ready. One walked up to me and asked, "What is the Army doing here?"

The UMP is a magazine fed submachine gun firing from a closed bolt. The UMP is chambered for .45 ACP to provide more stopping power against unarmored targets. The .45 ACP cartridges produce a lot of recoil, and make control difficult in full automatic. The cyclic fire rate is 600 rounds per minute.

I had already pulled out my Glock and it was on my lap ready to use. Jones cocked the big 50 getting ready to fire if ordered to do so.

I replied, "We are on a confidential mission. What are you Feds doing here?"

Presidential Order 13603. We suggest you do not interfere, mind your own business, and just move along."

"You know Order 13603 is a violation of the US Constitution and the Army believes it's an act of treason. Why are you taking the guns away from these people and their money? They're just trying to stay alive."

"You Army guys better leave now or there's going to be trouble. You know you look familiar to me. What's your name?"

"My name is Jack Gunn, what's your name?"

"I am Special Agent Fellows, the Agent in Charge here and I am the one asking the questions not you. I am the Boss man here."

The FBI agent pulled out his smart phone and was checking something … then he said, "You are Jack Gunn? Jack Gunn was killed by al-Qaida according to this."

"That's another Jack Gunn."

"No this is your picture here and there is an arrest warrant out on you for the murder of Aalee Abdual."

Agent Fellows was slowly raising is right hand to the trigger of his UMP45 so I pulled out my Glock sticking it in his face and said, "Don't touch that gun Fellows or I will blow your head off. That is a bull shit warrant because Aalee was wanted for terrorist acts against the US government. I killed him in self defense.

Fifty people saw it happen."

"It doesn't say anything in here about that."

Willis told his Rangers on the radio, "Heads up men be ready to rock and roll." Rock and roll means be ready to shoot on full automatic fire.

Willis got out of the Humvee, and walked over to Agent Fellows pointing his M 4 right in his face and advised him, "Agent Fellows we do not want any trouble here. Mr. Gunn is under the protection of the Army Rangers so there isn't any way you or anyone else is going to arrest him.

"We have you out gunned and out manned. Now have your men all lay down their weapons and take 50 steps backwards or we are going to open fire. Put down all your weapons including hand guns. You got 10 seconds to do so."

Agent Fellows ordered his men to lay down their guns and move back 50 steps. SPC Jones and SFC Kang walked around and collected the guns throwing them in a pile. By this time people started coming over and a crowd was gathering on the side of the road.

They started to chant, "Kill those Feds, kill those Feds, kill those Feds!"

SGM (Sergeant Major) Willis yelled to the crowd, "Anyone who had a gun or money taken by these guys go in their trucks and take them back. If anyone wants a new gun take one of those in the pile."

The crowd yelled, "Go Army!"

Agent Fellows shouted, "You can't do that these people will kill us!"

"Agent Fellows, you reap what you sow. We're leaving now so good luck," Willis told him.

Speaking to the crowd again Willis said, "We are leaving these Feds under your control so be nice to them."

Willis looking at me and then at the four black GMC SUVs and asked, "Jack why don't you take these. They are fully armored and you can always use a good vehicle, these are almost new."

I thought about it for a minute and replied, "Good idea Willis, it maybe stealing but when I think about all the tax money we have paid over the years it is only fair that the Feds donate these trucks to Tocabaga. Besides that they screwed me out of my social security money.

"Tommy you drive one, I'll drive one, Amy,

143

and Tony you each drive one. At least we won't go home empty handed. Willis you ride with me."

We stood there and watched as the agents ran down the road with a crowd of people chasing them. A few minutes later we heard gun fire, a lot of gun fire. I don't think the Feds ran fast enough to get away.

I said to Willis, "I guess they didn't play nice with the Feds."

Kang laughed and replied, "The stinking Feds got what they deserved. They were going to arrest you Jack."

"I wasn't worried about it."

"Oh and why not?"

"I wasn't worried because I am under the protection of the United States Army Rangers, the best fighting force in the world.

"You know what we should do … we should come back to Ellenton sometime and help these people set up a proper security defense. Organize them into a real fighting force for their own good."

Kang replied, "That's a good idea count me in but right now I just want to get back to the Fort."

"When we get back the drinks are on me."

Everyone laughed because drinks are always free on Tocabaga.

"Wait a minute I got a brain storm! Let's go ask some people at Ellenton if they have a tractor for sale or know where one is."

Maggie replied, "Good idea Jack, let's go."

Willis, Maggie, Amy, Tommy, and I went to the mall, while the others remained guarding the trucks. There were several hundred people milling around there. People had taken over the shops and stores and made them their homes.

As we walked around most people stayed away from us. After asking a few dozen people if anyone had a tractor for sale, one man told me go see Farmer John and pointed to an old man wearing shabby clothes sitting in a corner by himself, so I walked up to him.

His face was weather beaten, his eyes were gray and had dark circles under them, and he had on a straw hat with torn old blue jeans. I thought this guy was a farmer. He sat there watching us walk up to him and he had a concerned look on his face.

I said, "Hello my name is Jack Gunn and we are from Tocabaga. We're here looking to buy a tractor, do you know anyone who has a tractor for sale or where we can find one?"

The old man who looked hungry held out his hand and said, "Yep, I know where one is but it will cost you one hundred bucks."

I laughed a little and reached in my pocket and pulled out the hundred saying, "Here's the hundred my friend. Where's the tractor?"

He answered, "It's at my farm down the street. You got a car I'll take you there."

I thought we could trust this old guy he looks harmless so I told Amy to bring up a truck. We all got into the truck and drove to his little farm was just down the road off a side street about one mile away.

Arriving there I asked him, "What are you doing at the Mall when you have this nice little house and farm?"

He proceeded to tell me a sad story … his wife passed away, and then his two boys were killed. He ran out of money and couldn't pay his taxes so the government took his farm. A gang came to his house beat him up and made him leave. He hadn't been back to his house in almost a year.

He's too old to farm now so he sits at the mall begging for money or food, because it's safer there being around other people.

The Poor old man worked his whole life and now has nothing and no one to help him. I thought he's coming with us to Tocabaga. We can put him up and he can probably teach Maggie a thing or two about farming.

He opened the barn door and Maggie said, "This is a great tractor. Mr. ... what's your name?

"My name is Mr. Johnson, but most people call me Farmer John."

Maggie looking around in the barn found everything we needed and told Farmer John, "We will buy everything the trailer, tiller, plow, loader, and mower. How does $50,000 sound?"

Farmer John answered quickly, "It's a deal." He shook hands with Maggie.

I butted in, "Mr. Johnson we live on Tocabaga, you know where old Fort Desoto is, right over the Skyway. We are now part of an Army Ranger base and we could sure use your help. If you agree to come with us we will give you a free place to live, free food and security for the rest of your life."

"I was in the Army a long time ago but what do you want from an old fart like me?"

"We only ask you to teach us about farming and help Maggie run our farm."

The old man bent his head down and I heard him whisper, "Thank you God for sending these people to me."

Farmer John looked at me; he looked at all of us with a tear in his eye and said, "I got nothing left here … so when do we leave?"

I said, "We're leaving as soon as the trailer is hooked up."

Tommy and Willis had just finished hooking up the trailer to the F 350 and a car pulled in the driveway and sped toward us at the barn, slamming on the brakes two guys jumped out and yelled, "Hey what the hell you doing? This is our property!"

Willis and Tommy pulled their guns out of the truck and I put my hand on the Glock. Both men had side arms visible. One man had black hair and was medium built and the other had a bald head and was slightly bigger, around six feet tall. They looked to be about thirty years old.

Farmer John said, "This is the gang that beat me up and took my house."

I quickly drew my Glock, pointing it at them, and told them, "Ok boys carefully take out your guns, throw them over here at my feet and raise your hands." They complied with my order.

Willis and Tommy had them covered as I walked over to them and said, "So you tough guys beat up an old man and took his house ... well ... that don't sound tough to me. Let me tell you something I hate bullies and every time I meet one I beat the shit out of them or kill'em."

The jerk with black hair standing there with his hands in the air spoke up, "I didn't beat him up. I would never hit an old man. Don here is the one who beat up the old man."

"Mr. Johnson is that correct?"

"Yes that bald headed fellow beat me up."

"Since I am such a good guy we are going to let you off easy this time. Don come over here and bend over."

As he bent over I hit him in the head with the

149

barrel of my gun just hard enough to knock him to his knees. He shouted out in pain, "You're crazy."

I grabbed him by the right ear so he couldn't move, pulled out my Cold Steel fighting knife, and cut off his ear in one easy slice. It was like cutting soft butter and he screamed as blood ran all over his face.

I kicked him hard in the face knocking him down and told him, "Now every time you look in the mirror remember what you did to this old man, and never ever forget that Jack Gunn cut your fucking ear off."

Holding his ear I yelled into it, "Do you understand?"

The stupid shit shook his head yes, so I told him, "Open your mouth shit head!"

I gave him his bloody ear back by cramming it into his mouth.

Looking in his eyes I warned him, "I'll give you one day to get out of this house and out of Ellenton area. We'll be back here tomorrow and if you're still here we'll kill you on the spot. You got that shit head?"

Once again he shook his head yes which made me feel good.

I told everyone, "Ok we're done here let's go home and get that drink." We picked up their guns and drove away with our tractor, after we shot out all the tires on their car.

Coming to Route 75 we stopped to tell the Sheriff Deputies about the Feds at the Mall. They told us the Feds were always coming around but they were under orders not to interfere with them. The Deputies liked the fact that we took the Feds wheels. We didn't tell them that the people at Ellenton might have killed the Feds.

I told them my plan to come back to Ellenton and help these people learn how to protect themselves. The Deputies supported that idea and wanted to help in any way possible. Deputy Johnson gave me is cell phone number and told me to call him when a date is set.

We made it back to Tocabaga without any more problems. It goes to show you anything can happen out there it is a crazy nasty world. Everyone was surprised that we came back with four new trucks donated by the government and a great tractor.

Amy and Maggie found an empty condo and got

Mr. Johnson settled and then showed him around Camp Tocabaga. He was now looking happy and he couldn't wait to start work on the farm. Mr. Johnson now had something to live for, being a farmer again. We paid him his $50,000 but he refused to take it, and told us to save it for him.

I was at home and happy to be there writing these chronicles when it occurred to me that the Fed trucks probably have a GPS locator system and they could trace those vehicles to Tocabaga. I will have to ask Willis if someone can disconnect them however it maybe to late as they were most likely tracking us all along. That means we may have another run in with the Feds.

They will probably try to say we killed the FBI and ATF agents since we took their trucks. Then I thought if someone goes to the pig farm and sees the bloody mess there we could be in more trouble.

It never ends, you try to do something good and shit happens.

That's all for now, may God Bless America.

Jack Gunn, tocabaga.jack@gmail.com

DRAMATIS PERSONAE

TOCABAGA 3

WARM BLOOD – COLD STEEL

Amy – Daughter of Jack Gunn, a Nurse and sharp shooter

Chris – Handy man and Tocabaga security agent

Colonel Turner – Commanding Officer of the Army Rangers based at Fort Desoto

Captain Sessions – Combat officer, commands and controls combat operations in the field

Captain Clark – Chopper pilot

Captain Riley – Lady tank commander, girl friend of Captain Sessions

Eddy – Good Friend of Jack Gunn, brews beer and grows pot and is on the security team

Hemmi – Wife of Jack Gunn.

Johnny Evans - Little boy who found Captain Sessions

Jimmy Evans – Brother to Jimmy

Joan - Wife of Ron Gunn, a Nurse.

Jim Bo – Husband to Amy and Son-in Law of Jack.

Kendra – Granddaughter of Jack Gunn, Daughter of Tommy Gunn

Kane – Tocabaga trouble maker

Maggie – Wife of Robbie, who is in charge of the farming

Master Sergeant Kang – Army Ranger

Mr. Johnson or Famer John – Old time Farmer

Mr. Horn – Pig farmer and dirt bag

Robbie – Best friend of Jack Gunn, a Tocabaga security guard killed by the FPF on April 27, 2025

Ron - Brother of Jack Gunn retired Navy Veteran.

Rick – President of Tocabaga association, security team member

Rahim – A Muslim friend who moved to Tocabaga, with his family

Sergeant Major Willis – Ranger squad leader and security guard for Jack

Sergeant Cain – the Drone Master

Sergeant Smith - Army Ranger assigned as security guard for Jack

Shanda – Little girl, daughter of big Jim a bad guy, killed by Jack

Tommy Gunn – Son of Jack Gunn and a retired Marine Scout Sniper.

Tonya – Wife of Tommy Gunn

Tony – Bar keeper and sharp shooter for Tocabaga security.

www.ingramcontent.com/pod-product-compliance
Lightning Source LLC
Chambersburg PA
CBHW051522170626
46811CB00002B/950